A King Production presents...

Stackin'
Paper

A Novel

Joy Deja King

This novel is a work of fiction. Any references to real people, events, establishments, or locales are intended only to give the fiction a sense of reality and authenticity. Other names, characters, and incidents occurring in the work are either the product of the author's imagination or are used fictitiously, as those fictionalized events and incidents that involve real persons. Any character that happens to share the name of a person who is an acquaintance of the author, past or present, is purely coincidental and is in no way intended to be an actual account involving that person.

ISBN 10: 0975581112
ISBN 13: 978-0975581117
Cover concept by Joy Deja King & www.MarionDesigns.com
Cover layout and graphic design by: www.MarionDesigns.com
Typesetting: Linda Williams
Editor: Dolly Lopez

Library of Congress Cataloging-in-Publication Data;
King, Joy Deja

Stackin' Paper: a novel by Joy Deja King
For complete Library of Congress Copyright info visit;
www.joydejaking.com

A King Production
P.O. Box 912, Collierville, TN 38027

A King Production and the above portrayal log are trademarks of A King Production LLC

Dedication

This Book is Dedicated To My:

Family, Readers and Supporters. I LOVE you guys so much.
Please believe that!!

Chapter One
A Killer Is Born

Philly, 1993

"Please, Daquan, don't hit me again!" the young mother screamed, covering her face in defense mode. She hurriedly pushed herself away from her predator, sliding her body on the cold hardwood floor.

"Bitch, get yo' ass back over here!" he barked, grabbing her matted black hair and dragging her into the kitchen. He reached for the hot skillet from the top of the oven, and you could hear the oil popping underneath the fried chicken his wife had been cooking right before he came home. "Didn't I tell you to have my food ready on the table when I came home?"

"I... I... I was almost finished, but you came home early," Teresa stuttered, "Ouch!" she yelled as her neck damn near snapped when Daquan gripped her hair even tighter.

"I don't want to hear your fuckin' excuses. That's what yo' problem is. You so damn hard headed and neva want to listen. But like they say, a hard head make fo' a soft ass. You gon' learn to listen to me."

"Please, please, Daquan, don't do this! Let me finish frying your chicken and I'll never do this again. Your food will be ready and on the table everyday on time. I promise!"

"I'm tired of hearing your damn excuses."

"Bang!" was all you heard as the hot skillet came crashing down on Teresa's head. The hot oil splashed up in the air, and if Daquan hadn't moved forward and turned his head, his face would've been saturated with the grease.

But Teresa wasn't so lucky, as the burning oil grazed her hands, as they were protecting her face and part of her thigh.

After belting out in pain from the grease, she then noticed blood trickling down from the open gash on the side of her forehead. But it didn't stop there. Daquan then put the skillet down and began kicking Teresa in her ribs and back like she was a diseased infected dog that had just bitten him.

"Yo', Pops, leave moms alone! Why you always got to do this? It ain't never no peace when you come in this house." Genesis stood in the kitchen entrance with his fists clenched and panting like a bull. He had grown sick and tired of watching his father beat his mother down almost every single day. At the age of eleven he had seen his mother receive more ass whippings than hugs or any indication of love.

"Boy, who the fuck you talkin' to? You betta get yo' ass back in your room and stay the hell outta of grown people's business."

"Genesis, listen to your father. I'll be alright. Now go

back to your room," his mother pleaded.

Genesis just stood there unable to move, watching his mother and feeling helpless. The blood was now covering her white nightgown and she was covering her midsection, obviously in pain trying to protect the baby that was growing inside of her. He was in a trance, not knowing what to do to make the madness stop. But he was quickly brought back to reality when he felt his jaw almost crack from the punch his father landed on the side of his face.

"I ain't gon' tell you again. Get yo' ass back in your room! And don't come out until I tell you to! Now go!" Daquan didn't even wait to let his only son go back to his room. He immediately went over to Teresa and picked up where he left off, punishing her body with punches and kicks. He seemed oblivious to the fact that not only was he killing her, but also he was killing his unborn child right before his son's eyes.

A tear streamed down Genesis's face as he tried to reflect on one happy time he had with his dad, but he went blank. There were no happy times. From the first moment he could remember, his dad was a monster.

All Genesis remembered starting from the age of three was the constant beat downs his mother endured for no reason. If his dad's clothes weren't ironed just right, then a blow to the face. If the volume of the television was too loud, then a jab here. And, God forbid, if the small, two-bedroom apartment in the drug-infested building they lived in wasn't spotless, a nuclear bomb would explode in the form of Daquan. But the crazy part was, no matter how clean their apartment was or how good the food was cooked and his clothes being ironed just right, it was never good enough. Daquan would bust in the door, drunk or high, full of anger, ready to take out all his frustration out on his wife. The dead end jobs, being broke, living in the drug infested and violent prone city of Philadelphia had turned the already troubled man into poison to his whole family.

"Daddy, leave my mom alone," Genesis said in a calm, unemotional tone. Daquan kept striking Teresa as if he didn't hear his son. "I'm not gonna to tell you again. Leave my mom alone." This time Daquan heard his son's warning but seemed unfazed.

"I guess that swollen jaw wasn't enough for you. You dying to get that ass beat." Daquan looked down at a now black and blue Teresa who seemed to be about to take her last breath. "You keep yo' ass right here, while I teach our son a lesson." Teresa reached her hand out with the little strength she had left trying to save her son. But she quickly realized it was too late. The sins of the parents had now falling upon their child.

"Get away from my mother. I want you to leave and don't ever come back."

Daquan was so caught up in the lashing he had been putting on his wife that he didn't even notice Genesis retrieving the gun he left on the kitchen counter until he had it raised and pointed in his direction. "Lil' fuck, you un lost yo' damn mind! You gon' make me beat you with the tip of my gun."

Daquan reached his hand out to grab the gun out of Genesis's hand, and when he moved his leg forward, it would be the last step he'd ever take in his life. The single shot fired ripped through Daquan's heart and he collapsed on the kitchen floor, dying instantly.

Genesis was frozen and his mother began crying hysterically.

"Oh dear God!" Teresa moaned, trying to gasp for air. "Oh, Genesis baby, what have you done?" She stared at Daquan, who laid face up with his eyes wide open in shock. He died not believing until it was too late that his own son would be the one to take him out this world.

It wasn't until they heard the pounding on the front door that Genesis snapped back to the severity of the situation at hand.

"Is everything alright in there?" they heard the older lady from across the hall ask.

Genesis walked to the door still gripping the .380-caliber semi-automatic. He opened the door and said in a serene voice, "No, Ms. Johnson, everything is *not* alright. I just killed my father."

****

Two months later, Teresa cried as she watched her son being taking away to spend a minimum of two years in a juvenile facility in Pemberton, New Jersey.

Although it was obvious by the bruises on both Teresa and Genesis that he acted in self defense, the judge felt that the young boy having to live with the guilt of murdering his own father wasn't punishment enough. He concluded that if Genesis didn't get a hard wake up call, he would be headed on a path of self destruction. He first ordered him to stay at the juvenile facility until he was eighteen. But after pleas from his mother, neighbors and his teacher, who testified that Genesis had the ability to accomplish whatever he wanted in life because of how smart and gifted he was, the judge reduced it to two years, but only if he demonstrated excellent behavior during his time there. Those two years turned into four and four turned into seven. At the age of eighteen when Genesis was finally released he was no longer a young boy, he was now a criminal minded man.

Chapter Two
The Come Up

Philly, 2008

Every true hustler has asked themselves this question at least once in their life: How much money can I make and how long do I have to make it? Because in street life, one thing is for certain, time is never on your side. The more paper you can stack, the faster you can get out. But unfortunately it never seems to work out that way. The game is like the mob, baby. Once you're in, you're in.

****

Genesis patiently waited in his non-descript black 1990 Honda Civic parked across the street, watching a house on

30th Street near McKean. He'd been holding court everyday for the last month, scoping the place out.

As the sun began to set, Genesis thought about what put him in the possible sticky situation. Word on the blocks was that the two cats that robbed him rested their heads at the spot. He was always told that revenge is best served cold and he hoped that was the case with the dudes that decided to rape him of his hard earned cash and newly purchased drugs.

He continued to observe the comings and goings. Within the last month he noticed a few things. He had never seen a female on the premises. The traffic coming through the front door was limited. Besides the two dudes who were there on a regular basis, only one other guy had come over, and he always carried the same black duffel bag with him. When he arrived it would be bulging, and when he'd leave it was flat. So Genesis figured he was either carrying a lot of money, drugs or both. If he believed the talk on the streets, the three of them were a one team robbing machine, raping dealers for cash and drugs.

As he took a long drag from his Newport, Genesis felt his cell vibrate. "What's good?"

"You tell me, man. Where you at?" his right-hand man, Deuce questioned.

"Still babysitting."

"Yo, I think you may need to leave that shit alone and take an L on it."

"You trippin'! I can't take no more loses. I've been grindin' on these streets for a minute now, and when I'm finally starting to make a come up, these clown as niggas want to rape me for my shit. Fuck that! I've been busting my ass for years and because of those cats I ain't got nothin' to show for it."

"Genesis, I understand your hostility. Shit I'm pissed too, but I don't want you to get caught out there with them niggas."

"Why the fuck you think I've been babysitting for all these weeks? At this point I can pretty much calculate when those motherfuckers take a shit."

"Man, you crazy."

"Yeah, you right, I am. Soon them niggas about to really see what crazy look like. They picked the wrong nigga to jack. I'm too thirsty to tolerate this shit."

"Why don't I come over there and sit with you, keep you company."

Genesis knew his friend was worried about him but he didn't want any company or distractions. "Nah, I'm straight. The two of them is leaving the house now so I'ma head home and handle some other business."

"Cool. So I'll see you over on the block later tonight?"

"No doubt." Genesis flipped his phone closed and didn't think twice at the fact he lied to his best friend. He did so for his own protection. He didn't want Deuce involved in what was about to go down. This was his problem and he would be the one to deal with it.

Instead of the two dudes leaving like he told Deuce, they were actually coming and Genesis watched as they carried two large bags into the house. After they went inside, Genesis waited another ten minutes before putting his plan into action.

He pulled up the black hoodie to cover his caramel-colored bald head, and grabbed the 9mm and ski mask from his glove compartment before exiting the car. As he tossed the still burning cigarette into the middle of the street, he remained fixated on one agenda; getting his shit back.

With the sun completely down and day turning to night it was the perfect time for Genesis to make his move. The street was completely dead and no one noticed him creeping to the side of the house.

Earlier that day while the robbing crew was out handling their business, Genesis did a quick but precise check of every inch outside of the house. He knew there was a small window on the side of the house that gave a clear view of the movements inside.

He knelt down and put his back against the bricks, eyeing the activities of the two men. They were in a bedroom counting the stacks of money they collected that day. "Damn, them niggas gettin' paper!" Genesis mumbled under his breath. He could hear them laughing and joking as they counted the next man's cash:

"Did you see that motherfucker's face when I told him to get down on his knees like he be having his bitch do when he want some head?" the short light skinned man popped.

"Yeah, that nigga was shook. For a minute he thought you were gon' tell him to suck your dick off. It took all my strength not to bust out laughing on that clown," the tall brown skinned man with long braids said.

"I know, I peeped that shit too. I wanted to tell him ain't no homo shit this way. But the fuckin' fear in his eyes was priceless. He was more worried about me telling him to suck my dick than stealing his loot. He seemed happier than a motherfucker for us to take his shit and bounce."

"You ain't lying. I had no idea Rashawn was making paper like that. I thought that dude was clocking minor figures, but he had to have gotten over a hundred g's from his crib, plus that heroin. Like my man Ice Cube say, 'Today was a good day',"

Both the men gave each other a pound, relishing in their come up of the day.

Genesis stood there shaking his head. *I can't believe they got my man, Rashawn. These niggas is straight grimy. Yeah, it's time they got shut the fuck down.*

He scanned the room and noticed they had their artillery on the dresser, but then when they sat down on the bed to finish counting the money, each took the gun off that was in the back of their pants and tossed it on the bed.

After about another hour, they finally finished counting the money and headed to the living room area that was off to the side. From his angle he could see one of the cats sitting on a chair and holding the remote control, but he couldn't get a view where he was. He got an idea by watching the direction the light-skinned dude would turn his head and direct his conversation.

The tall brown-skinned dude with braids then walked across the room, and after a few minutes came back with two Heinekens and what looked to be weed, so Genesis assumed he had went into the kitchen.

After about another twenty minutes, when it seemed both men had gotten comfortable and had a buzz, Genesis figured it was time to make his move. He hoped that the weapons they left in the bedroom were all they had and they would be defenseless the same way he was when they robbed him.

It was now pitch black outside and Genesis put on his ski mask as he made his way to the front door. At six-two and two hundred and ten pounds of solid muscle, he used all his strength to kick down the door.

The two dudes were so high and caught off guard that they barely had time to react. Genesis knew that the short dude was on his left hand side, sitting in the chair and he was the first one to catch a bullet right between his eyes. The second cat quickly snapped out of his weed and beer induced high and jumped out of his seat headed to the bedroom to get his own protection. But he was one step too slow. Genesis busted off three shots that penetrated his neck and upper and lower back. He fell face forward, crashing his head against the glass cocktail table.

Genesis didn't waste any time and went straight into action. He ran into the bedroom, grabbed all the money off the bed and started stuffing into the big duffel bag on the floor. As he rushed trying to get all the money as quickly as possible, he dropped a couple of stacks on the floor. When he bent down to pick them up his hand knocked against a hard piece of metal. Upon further inspection he noticed five big silver metal cases. He opened one and it was full of twenty and one hundred dollar bills. Genesis started pulling all the cases out. Three were full of cash and the other two were full of drugs. "I know these motherfuckers weren't keeping they stash underneath the fuckin' bed! What type of shit is this?" he asked out loud.

"I can't carry all this shit out in one pop. Damn, this a lot of shit. But with all this loot and product, I can go from nothin' to somethin' overnight," Genesis reasoned as he talked the situation out loud hoping it would help him figure out what to do.

"Shit, I know somebody must of heard them shots go off

and they probably already called the police. Then that third nigga that be bringing shit over here could pop up at any moment. Let me just take what I can carry now and get the fuck outta here."

The cases were heavy as fuck, so Genesis carried the duffel bag on his back and was able to carry three of the cases. He scrammed out of the house with his eyes darting in every direction, making sure he wasn't on anybody's radar. Once he put the bag and suitcases in his trunk and got back in the car, he put the key in the ignition. But he stopped. He looked back at the house, then scanned the neighborhood again.

"Fuck that! I need all that shit!" He leaped out of the car and ran back to the house. He went to the bedroom grabbed the other two suitcases and the fucking guns before breaking out.

****

That night, Genesis lay on his bed counting every dollar he confiscated. There was over seven hundred thousand dollars in those suitcases, not including the hundred and thirty-five thousand in the duffel bag. There was also 20 pounds of 85 percent pure heroin. "I can't believe my fuckin' luck! I go there to take back the fifty thousand dollars and one key of heroin them niggas yanked from me and hit the motherfuckin' jackpot. That's what's up!"

Genesis didn't get any sleep that night. He turned his cell off and sat up constructing a plan in his head to turn his jackpot into a multi-million dollar drug business. Between the cash and the drugs, he already had over a million, which was more than enough to build a mini drug empire, but he knew he had to be smart and careful about how he flipped the cash and product.

The first thing he decided to do was get a bullshit apartment that he would never chill at to put the money and drugs. He also thought it best to invest in a safe so if anybody did come up in his crib, they wouldn't be able to open the shit up.

As Genesis continued to strategize, the reality of his new found fortune was kicking in. He had spent many days and nights when he was caged up in juvenile detention, wishing for a better life. For the first year he was locked down his mother would come to see him every weekend. There was only one month his mother stayed away, and that was because she gave birth to his little sister. Genesis understood and was thrilled when she finally came back to visit and brought the baby. He immediately fell in love with the beautiful little girl. Touching her tiny hands gave him hope and motivation to behave while locked up because he had someone to come home to that he felt needed him. With their father dead he never wanted his sister to lack for the love or attention that he never got from his father while growing up.

"Mom, you still haven't told me her name," Genesis remembered saying to his mother.

"It's Genevieve. Now I have two precious babies, Genesis and Genevieve. I know you're going to be a wonderful big brother to her. You only got one more year to go so be on your best behavior so you can come on home. We need you, me and Genevieve."

"I promise. I won't get in any trouble. I'm going to come home and be the man of the house. Take care of my family. I've been doing real good in the classes I'm taking, so good that I'm actually taking advance courses. One of my teachers said if I continue to make the grades I'm making he'll see about putting me in this special program for gifted students. Nobody here has ever qualified for the program. But he believes I can ace the test and get in."

"I'm so proud of you, son. I always knew you were special. I didn't need no teacher or some test to let me know. You're going to grow up to be somebody important. You just wait and see."

Teresa stood up and gave Genesis a kiss goodbye. He then kissed his little sister bye and one of the other inmates took a picture of the three of them with Teresa's camera. "I'll send you the picture in the mail so you can hang it up on your wall."

"Thanks, Mom. I'll see you next weekend, right?"

"Of course, baby. I wouldn't miss seeing you for nothing in the world. I love you."

"I love you too, Mama."

Genesis smiled as he watched his mother walk out the facility with his sister. It was the last time he would ever see them again during his duration at the juvenile detention. When his mother missed the first weekend he figured the baby must've had gotten sick and she couldn't make it. When he tried to call, no one answered the phone. Then when the second and third weekend passed he began to worry but tried to keep himself busy with schoolwork. After two months with no word he received a letter from his mother:

Dear Genesis,

I love you very much and always will. I pray for you everyday and will continue to do so. I know its hard being locked away in that place, but you're a soldier and I want you to continue to be strong. Focus on taking care of yourself and don't worry about me and Genevieve.

I finally met a good man who wants to take good care of me and your sister. The thing is he lives down south so we're going to have to move. So I won't be able to come see you anymore. I know this must be difficult for you to understand, but when you get older you'll see how hard it is to be a single mother raising a child on your own. Good men are hard to come by and I want a better life for me and your sister.

Stay strong and I can't wait to see you when you get out. Once we get settled I'll send you a letter with our new address and phone number so you can contact me. I've enclosed that picture we took last time I was there. You look so handsome. I love you, baby.

Love Mom

That same day, Genesis received another letter saying that he had gotten accepted into the gifted program. But instead of rejoicing, he held the picture of him, his sister and mother in his hand and cried himself to sleep.

His mother never did send her new phone number and address, and Genesis never did start the gifted program. Once he realized his mother and sister was gone, he felt all alone and totally shut down. He was no longer motivated to get out so he could be with his family. Instead he began bonding with the other troubled young men in the facility. From that day forward, excelling in school wasn't even a thought. Riding a wave of destruction took center stage.

Chapter Three
Da Dopeman

It had been less than three months, and Genesis was swiftly seeing his dreams come to fruition. He sat back for a few weeks and let the street buzz surrounding the murders of the two cats from the robbing crew die down before making his mark. Luckily the cats had fucked over so many people that nobody really cared who took them off the streets. Most felt a well-needed service had been done. Plus, with the "no snitch" rule that resonated strongly in Philly and the city more concerned about the killing of their own police officers, two bad asses known for causing havoc was thrown in the pile with the rest of the menace-to-society criminals. Genesis still wasn't taking any chances. He didn't want to deal with any retaliation at the moment because he was too driven to make moves with his new product. Playing low had paid off, and now he was next in line to being "that nigga" in Philly.

****

"Yo, is you taking that flight with me to ATL or what?" Genesis asked Deuce as they drove down N. Broad Street.

"When you leaving?"

"Tomorrow morning."

"I don't know. I'm supposed to be hooking up with this shorty tomorrow night."

Genesis gripped the steering wheel on his newly purchased Range and paused making sure he heard his man correctly.

"Hold up, man. I must be trippin' because I thought I heard you say that you can't go to ATL because you checking for some trick."

"Listen here. Tonya ain't no trick."

"Nigga, please. That's all you fuck wit'. Every chick I un seen you wit' got trick written all over them. But that's on you. But when it start interfering with business, then that's on me, which means we got a problem."

"All you every talk about anymore is business and making money. It seems like yesterday we was laughing and joking. Now you always serious. I don't know if I'm really feeling this whole new 'Nino Brown' aura you got going on. Shit, next thing I know you might be putting that sword through my hand like he did to fuckin' Christopher Williams's character."

"You got jokes. But seriously, I need you in Atlanta with

me. While the money is hot we need to get all we can."

"Man, I'm still trying to figure out how all of sudden you blew the fuck up. It's like you came into an endless supply of heroin or some shit."

"I told you. My new connect hooked me up. And his product is official. But that shit is about to dry up, that's why I need to meet with this new connect in Atlanta. I heard they shit is the business too, but I don't know these cats like that, so I need you for backup."

"I feel you. That pussy can wait, even though that shit is good. And I'm not gonna even talk about the brain that broad give. The more I think about it, let's hurry up and get the fuck back. I don't want Tonya giving that pussy to nobody else."

"Whatever, man. Let's just go handle this business."

****

When Genesis and Deuce arrived at the Hartsfield-Jackson International Airport in Atlanta, they were both anxious, but for two different reasons. Deuce was fiending to get back to Philly so he could twist his new piece, Tonya out, and Genesis was praying his new connect was on the up and up so his expanding cash flow could continue.

Nobody on the streets knew it, including Deuce, but Genesis was completely wiped out of the twenty pounds of heroin he confiscated from the now deceased robbers. And in all actuality, because of the purity of the heroin being such a high percentage, he was able to cut it up and almost double the weight, but his product moved like water on the street.

After watching the "American Gangster" movie, Genesis had always told himself that if he ever came upon the right product, he would brand it like his man, Frank Lucas did when he was running the streets of Harlem. So when he realized how potent his shit was, he named it Hot As Ice. After giving a few freebies to some local junkies who were his loyal customers, word soon spread that Hot As Ice was the business, and that's all everybody was checking for. He derived the name because the junkies told him that the first hit was hot going through their blood streams, and it was so powerful that it felt as it their veins were frozen like ice.

Before Genesis could blink, his stash was nil. The problem wasn't re-upping on some new product, it was finding some that was fire. After branding his goods, he had to maintain the quality his customers had come to expect. So when one of the local dealers told him he heard that a cat in Atlanta had the bomb shit, Genesis instantly jumped on it knowing that time wasn't on his side.

"Damn, this airport big as shit! How long before we get to the shuttle?" Deuce complained as he dragged his carryon luggage.

"I told you to check that shit in. But we almost there. See, it's pulling up now."

Deuce threw his bags right on the floor, not even watching or caring if they hit anybody already standing on the shuttle. "It's about time! I thought I was gonna pass out."

"Man, you trippin'. You better hit that gym and stop whining like a baby," Genesis said, teasingly patting Deuce's slightly protruding belly.

"Fuck you! My shit is good. A woman likes to hold on to

a little something-something. I can't help it if a nigga eating good. I'ma have to put that on my baby's mom. You know she can lay it down in the kitchen."

"Which one? You got three. But, whatever, like I said, you need to hit that gym and tone your shit up."

"So what? I can be cock-diesel like you? I'm good. I'm diesel in the only area that matter." Deuce looked down and slightly gripped his pants in the penis area. The elderly white woman standing beside him frowned and started moving to the other side of the shuttle. "Don't be afraid, grandma. You know you curious about that Mandingo meat."

"Yo, shut up!" Genesis chuckled, tapping Deuce upside the head. "You play too much."

"Shit, I wasn't playing. You know she probably frisky as hell, dying to get some good dick."

"Deuce, on the real, cut it out." Genesis could see the stares and glares they were getting, and one thing he didn't like was unwanted attention. He was relieved when the shuttle came to a stop and the doors opened. He knew with Deuce there was no shutting him up once he got started.

As they made their way to baggage claim, Genesis had a million thoughts running through his brain, and it all centered on business until something, or rather someone, made him stop in his tracks. "Damn!" was all he managed to let out at first.

"Man, I peeped her too. That bitch bad as hell. Do you see the ass and legs on that chick? She fine as a motherfucker, but definitely not my type."

"What you mean by that?" Genesis asked, because in his mind, a woman that fine was every man's type.

"You can't tell. She one of those high-class stuck-up

bitches. I mean look at her. She one of those chicks that like to show just enough to tease you but still want to cover up. I mean she got on that short ass dress that is accentuating her perfect ass and pretty legs, but then she want to put on a little school girl sweater trying to look innocent. And did you peep the pearls? Come on now! She definitely giving off that housewife-hooker vibe. Shit, I don't even think she got a weave. I think that might be her real hair. I don't have time for broads like that. They too high maintenance for me. I want my bitch to just have gotten off the pole—the stripper pole."

It took Genesis another five minutes to stop staring at the beauty who had him so intrigued he didn't realize his luggage had already gone by twice.

Upon further assessment, as he watched her get her luggage, he did know where his man Deuce was coming from. She was the type of young woman that exemplified class but was sexy as all fuck. From the peep toe pumps to the understated makeup, nothing was overdone but played up just enough to emphasize her best assets. Genesis wanted to walk over and introduce himself, but something held him back. Although he was now considered of the baller status, Genesis wasn't confidant that his hood-rich fame would measure up to lock down a woman like her.

"Man, stop drooling over there and go get your swagger on, and introduce yourself. I know you want to."

"Nah, I'm good. Her man probably outside waiting for her. Plus, this is a business trip. No time for socializing."

Genesis finally retrieved his luggage and continued to stare as the woman walked away.

"Look here. Either you gonna go chase after that puppy

or lick your wounds and keep it moving. But make up your mind because I'm ready to fuckin' go."

"Deuce, shut the fuck up! Let's go."

****

After picking up their SUV from Enterprise rental car, they hit I-85 and headed in the direction they were supposed to meet up with the connect. They were going to discuss prices, quantity and the location. Genesis would have his people pick up the product tomorrow. He figured if everything went smoothly, it would take no longer than a day, but he packed a few extra clothes to be prepared.

"Are we almost there, 'cause I'm hungry?" Deuce growled, rubbing his belly.

"We just got to Atlanta and all you've been doing is complaining. You worse than a woman. I shoulda left yo' ass back in Philly."

"Damn right! I wish you had. But nah, you my man and I gotta have your back. I'ma little irritable, you know how I get when I'm hungry."

"Well, we here now," Genesis said, pulling up into a parking lot off of Peachtree Street. He drove around to the back of the building like he was told to do, and saw a pearl white Bentley and a silver Ferrari parked in front of what looked to be a recording studio.

"You sure this the right spot?" Deuce questioned, sizing up the vehicles.

"This the address he gave me." Genesis glanced down at

the piece of paper he wrote the address down on to double check.

"I ain't mad at em'. If that's they whips, they got big shit poppin'."

"I heard here in Atlanta, him and his partner are the man. But we'll see once we get a hold of their product."

"Then lets do this," Deuce countered, stepping out of the passenger side. "But yo, I'm mad we ain't got no arsenal."

"Dude instructed me we couldn't bring none no way. He said they'll be searching us at the door, and if we got so much as a butter knife on us the deal was off."

"Word?" Deuce stood motionless, shocked by what Genesis said. "They paranoid like that?"

"Shit, the way the game is going these days I can't blame him. If we could've brought some heat I would've drove our asses up here."

"I thought you just didn't want to make that long ass drive. I feel you."

When Genesis and Deuce got to the front door, it was made of solid steel metal. Genesis looked up and nodded to Deuce to check out the cameras over their heads. Five seconds later, two big burly men that stood the same height as Genesis, but had about hundred and fifty pounds on him opened the door.

"Step inside," one of the strongly built men said, directing them to a closed off opening right outside another set of steel doors. The other man stood to the side holding a Heckler & Koch MP5 with his finger on the trigger, ready to blast.

Deuce swallowed hard, starting to feel a tad claustrophobic.

Genesis stood extra tall, appearing unruffled, but inside

he was hoping he hadn't walked into some bullshit.

The henchman patted Genesis and Deuce down then emptied their pockets. They remained silent knowing this was a part of the drill, but Genesis kept saying to himself, *This heroin better be the shit!* Once they passed the inspection, the next set of steel doors opened automatically.

The four men all remained quiet as they went up an elevator that let them off on the top floor. It seemed everywhere Genesis turned there was a camera clocking their every move.

"Stay here, I'll be back," the henchman ordered as the other henchman with the MP5 stood babysitting them.

They stood in the hallway for fifteen minutes until they were told they could come in. Both Genesis and Deuce were expecting to see a top-dollar plush layout, given the whips out front and the over-the-top security setup. But to their surprise, they entered an all black room, from the floor to the walls, with nothing but a black table and four chairs in the center.

"What the hell we un' walked into?" Deuce mumbled loud enough for Genesis to hear him. But it was if Deuce was reading his mind since Genesis was contemplating the same thing. Just then the doors in front of them opened and they did a double take.

"You fellas can have a seat, and while you're at it, you can close your mouths too."

"We were expecting to meet our connect. I'm assuming he got held up and you're here to keep us company until he arrives?" Genesis inquired, trying to sound diplomatic.

"You looking at your connect. I'm CoCo and this is my partner, Chanel."

Genesis and Deuce turned towards each other. The men were stunned that their connect was a pair of mocha chocolate identical twin beauties.

"This is either a mistake or a funny ass joke," Genesis reasoned. Because in his mind there was no way these two dime pieces that looked like they just stepped off a T.I. music video were balling at this level, especially in the drug game.

"Listen, we don't have time for mistakes or jokes. We running a business, a very lucrative one at that. So you can either sit down and handle yours, or Chuck will be more than happy to escort you back to your car."

"You're serious?" Genesis repeated, needing confirmation. "But I didn't talk to a female on the phone. I talked to a dude."

"Yeah, you spoke to Chuck. He's our middleman. He's the one that filters out the clowns from the legitimate business people, because as I said, we don't have time to waste. So what you doing, are you leaving or staying?"
CoCo put her hand on her tiny waist and leaned forward, putting the other hand against the table. Her 34 double D's seemed as if they were about to break free from the V-neck red silk blouse she was wearing. Her sister, Chanel remained mute but looking just as ravishing in the exact same outfit her sister was wearing, except her blouse was white. Dangling from their necks were iced out panthers with a pair of emeralds for eyes.

"Let's do this," Genesis finally said.

CoCo gave a slight grin as if she had been through this script before, and she had. It was forever the same way. Every man that walked up in there wanting to buy some dope assumed another man would be the supplier. They dick always went limp when the cats realized that the twins weren't eye-candy for them to lust after, but official bitches handling they business and deciding if they would sell them their product.

One pimp-acting cat from Detroit bust in the room and knew for a fact that the delectable twins were part of the welcoming committee and completely lost it when he realized they weren't for-hire whores. He actually pulled out his heat and threatened to blaze the place up if the head nigga in charge didn't show his face. Because of his foolishness, they instated the "no weapons" rule.

Most dealers in the game felt naked without their piece, and some refused to take the meeting thinking they'd be vulnerable to a setup. But as far as the twins were concerned, that was their loss. Their lives were too precious to gamble with people who were in a shady business to begin with. And furthermore, the clients they did have spent so much paper, it wasn't that serious for the clowns that didn't want to play.

"Cool. Have a seat. Would you fellas like a drink? We have a fully stocked bar in the back."

"I'll take a Hennessey," Deuce said, needing something to take the edge off.

"First, let's handle our business then we'll discuss drinks," Genesis interjected. He wanted them to have a clear head dealing with CoCo and Chanel. For two women to be at this high of a level, he knew they were on top of their shit and you couldn't be any less than a hundred percent when dealing with them.

"I'm digging your style. I appreciate a man who knows

how to prioritize."

CoCo always offered her new clients a drink first, and nine times out of ten they would accept. The revealing blouse, short skirt complimenting her long toned legs and the liquor was all a part of her game to lure the men in and put them on the offense. They would be so busy trying to control their hard-ons that she could throw all types of high ass prices in their faces and they would gladly say "yes", hoping some pussy would be the icing on the cake after the deal closed. But CoCo quickly recognized that she would have to shoot straight from the hip in her dealings with Genesis.

After about an hour or so of what seemed more like negotiations for a Wall Street takeover, both parties finally reached an agreement on prices, quantity and how each would be exchanged. At first, Genesis felt the dollar amount was a tad too high for him to make a huge profit. But when Chanel brought out a sample of the heroin and the liquid to test it's purity, he was sold. It had the exact same percentage he was pushing in the street now, so his brand, Hot As Ice, would remain intact.

"Damn, can I have that drink now?" Deuce blurted out after the deal was wrapped. Everybody in the room burst out laughing, including Chuck and the henchman with the MP5.

"No doubt. Speaking of drinks, do you fellas have plans for tonight?" CoCo inquired.

"Nah, we were gon' chill, maybe have some dinner."

"Well if you're up to it, a friend of mine is having a private party at the Velvet Room tonight. It's going to be on point. You guys should come as our guests. How 'bout it?"

"You good for it, Deuce?"

"Hell yeah! I need to let off some steam."

"Alright, so we'll pick you up about ten. I'll call you when we're on our way and let me know where you at. Oh, and fellas, the dress code is grown and sexy, so leave the Timbs at your hotel room."

"We got this," Genesis countered with a sexy smile, showing a full set of perfect white, straight teeth.

When Genesis and Deuce left the building they both stared at the two luxury cars they'd peeped when they first arrived, and then back at the building.

"You really think all this shit is them chicks? I mean real talk, because yo, these bitches are seriously ballin' if it is. I ain't neva ran across no broads making moves like this. They clocking major figures," Deuce said.

"I ain't saying shit until we get in the car. Knowing them chicks, they may have sound devices planted in the concrete," Genesis joked, but was dead serious.

When they got in the car and closed the door, Genesis sat back in his seat for a minute and put his hand over his mouth as if in deep thought. "That was some bizarre shit."

"Bizarre as fuck. I might know a couple of dudes that's making moves on those chicks' level, and two might be a stretch. I mean you've had a major come up these last few months and I know your money has to be long. But not only are they getting money, they must have a crazy connect. You asked them for fifty pounds and they didn't even sneeze. They getting dope with that purity level, that's power right there."

"And that's what I need—the power."

"Damn right! I know that dynamic duo ain't trying to give up they dopeman."

"True, but hopefully if I play my cards right I'll get it on my own."

Chapter Four

Excuse Me, Miss

When the Rolls Royce Limo turned off Chamblee Tucker Road into the parking lot of the Velvet Room, it resembled an exclusive car show with nothing but six figures and up extravagant vehicles. As the driver pulled up to the front entrance, Genesis observed what looked to be Atlanta's finest stepping through the glass door entrance.

Before the driver came around and opened their door, Genesis glanced across to where the twins were sitting to see if the package they were bringing tonight could compete with the high echelon females gracing the spot. He couldn't front, he was impressed at how tight their getups were pulled together. Both had on Bonnie four-inch high heel platform ankle strapped sandals with horse bit ring buckle details, and Gucci script logo on the front right bottom side. He assumed the scoop neck moro viscose jersey one piece was also Gucci, with CoCo rocking hers in absolute purple with metallic silver shoes, and Chanel in the mustard color version with metallic gold leather shoes. They stood an excellent chance of leaving with the "showstopper of the night" award.

Genesis also felt confidant in his attire which was a sand cotton twill cardigan shirt with matching tuxedo pants. A dark brown leather hidden belt buckle and sand suede calf zip boots accented by his diamond faced Franck Muller timepiece, and 2.5 karat diamond stud.

Deuce played it cool in some black slacks, shirt, Prada loafers and his double-sided diamond cross that he never took off.

"You, fellas, ready to do this?" CoCo asked, ready to get her party on.

"I been ready." Deuce gulped down the last of the champagne he was sipping.

"Ladies first." Genesis sat back, letting the twins make their exit first. He noticed all eyes staring in their direction, wanting to get a peek at who rolled up on the scene like they owned Atlanta. Clearly by the greetings the sisters received, if they didn't own Atlanta, people knew who they were as if they did. The four were escorted to a draped booth in the back that had a reserved sign on the table.

"Do you all want anything to drink besides the bubbly?" CoCo asked, as she told the hostess that seated them what she wanted.

"We straight. Who is this party for anyway? Mad people have come out to show 'em love." Genesis was curious to know. Not only did he see a few high profile athletes, but there were rappers, music moguls and a bevy of beautiful women decorating the place, he also recognized a few major players from the drug game he had did business with in the past.

"Arnez Douglass. He's a major player out here in *Hot*lanta."

"I can see. It seems like all the heavyweights are out supporting him."

"Pretty much anybody who is somebody in this town knows him, and if not they're jumping through hoops trying."

"Why is that?"

"Because Arnez is the one motherfucker that can make anything happen. If he hasn't, then it can't be done."

"Dude got power like that?"

CoCo locked eyes with Genesis, then smacked her lips and turned her head at his question as if saying, *"You figure it out"*. If CoCo was preaching the truth, Genesis wanted an up-close look at who this Arnez Douglass was.

As Genesis sipped on his champagne pondering if Arnez could be of any assistance with his business dealings, he almost choked on his drink as he zoomed in on a familiar face. He nudged Deuce's arm. "Is that shorty that we saw at the airport earlier today?" Genesis knew his eyes weren't deceiving him but wanted confirmation.

"Damn this a small world! I'd neva forget that pretty as bitch. Let me find out that's your soul mate," Deuced joked. "You better not chicken out this time. Go handle your business."

The woman was standing in front of a table as if waiting for someone. Genesis hoped she was waiting for a female and not her man. But at this point he didn't care. He didn't believe in coincidences and he felt there was a reason he had seen the same woman twice in one day at two totally different locations.

Without saying a word, he stood up and headed in the direction of the young lady that captured his eye. As he got closer he sized up the black silk crepe draped gown with a gold leather belt that cinched her waist and emphasized her hourglass figure. One side of her jet-black hair slightly swooped over her right eye, giving her angelic face a mysterious, naughty girl underlining.

As Genesis entered her space, without warning she turned in his direction and their bodies were within inches of each other. For a moment when she glanced up and their eyes met, Genesis forgot what he wanted to say.

"You startled me!" the woman said in a low voice.

"I'm sorry, that wasn't my intention. I noticed you as I was sitting down and wanted to introduce myself. I'm Genesis."

"Hi. Not to be rude but I'm here with my man."

"I understand. But just hear me out for a minute. What I'm about to say may sound like some BS, but it's real talk. I saw you earlier today at the airport. You were at the baggage claim area. I swear I was love struck—or make that infatuated—from the moment I laid eyes on you. And then when I saw you tonight at this party, I couldn't let you slip past me again without at least trying to get to know you."

"You really saw me today at the airport?"

"Yes. You had on a gray wrap dress with a black sweater, black open-toe heels and a string of pearls. Your hair was up, revealing the angle of your neck."

"I don't know whether to be scared or flattered."

"Never scared, only flattered. I wish you weren't here with your man but I learned at a very young age you can't have everything you want."

"How do you know I would even want you if I weren't here with my man?"

"Because you would've never stood here for this long and listened to me if you weren't interested. Plus, the eyes never lie."

"Maybe you're right, but I am here with my man and I need to go to him. Excuse me."

The woman walked away so fast that Genesis didn't even have a chance to get her name or say goodbye. He stood watching, trying to get a glance at the man who was lucky enough to call her theirs, but she disappeared into a crowd of people.

Genesis walked back to the table with a tinge of defeat. He wanted her, and it wasn't only because she was gorgeous, but something about her was drawing him in. Being locked up so long, he never experienced puppy love or even had a real girlfriend. He had fucked with a few chicks while he was out in the streets making money, but none of them meant more than just that, a fuck. In his mind, Genesis always envisioned himself making it to the top of his hustle with a certain caliber woman by his side. Thus far he had never met or seen her until now, and he wasn't ready to let it go.

When he sat back down at the table, CoCo was kicking it with a couple of cats. Deuce was putting his best pimp game on and Chanel remained mute in the corner seat. He didn't understand her role or what she did. She barely spoke two words, but CoCo never let Chanel leave her side, so Genesis knew she had some value and it went beyond being blood.

Before he could get comfortable, Genesis saw a man who looked to be black and Cuban walking towards the table with two bodyguards beside him. He was draped in a tailor-made pinstripe suit and had so much swagger in his walk you knew he had to be somebody because even a skilled perpetrator couldn't manufacture that aura.

"If it isn't the lovely CoCo. You know my party wouldn't have been complete if you hadn't showed up."

"Baby, you know I wouldn't have missed one of your bangers for nothing. And this is the most important one. It's your birthday."

"Happy birthday, Arnez!" the normally mute Chanel stood up and said before leaning over the table to give him a hug.

"Now I feel extremely important. I got the most beautiful set of twins on the southeast to come out and show me love."

This cat must really be the man if he got quiet ass Chanel to speak and stand up all in one pop, Genesis thought to himself.

"Arnez, I have a very special birthday gift for you," CoCo teased.

"Where is it? Give it to me. I love opening presents!"

"This present can't be opened. I take that back, it can be

opened, just in private." Arnez gave CoCo a strange look. "I know I sound crazy. But seriously, I met this drop dead gorgeous girl when I was in Miami a week ago that I know would be perfect for you. She's just your style. I wanted to bring her to the party tonight but her flight got cancelled because of weather conditions, but she'll be here tomorrow afternoon. Trust me, you'll love her."

"I do trust you, but I'm no longer on the market."

"Excuse me?" CoCo was obviously shocked by his admission. "When did this happen, and who is the woman that got you to settle down?"

"Her name is Talisa Washington, and I've been seeing her for a few months. I've finally gotten her to let me be her man. You have to meet her." Arnez looked around. "Go find Talisa and bring her to me," he told one of his bodyguards. "And who are your gentlemen friends?"

"My fault. I was so caught up in our conversation it made me rude. This is Genesis and Deuce. We're working on some business together. I wanted to show them a good time so of course I had to bring them to your joint." The three men nodded their heads at each other showing respect.

"This is a very nice party you're having here. And oh, happy birthday," Genesis added.

As the men shared small talk, they didn't notice the bodyguard heading back to the table until he whispered something in Arnez's ear. A few seconds later Arnez turned around to talk to someone, but you couldn't see who it was because of the height and weight of his bodyguard.

"This is my girlfriend, Talisa, Talisa, this is CoCo and her sister, Chanel."

"It's nice to meet you," Talisa said, smiling at the women.

"Talisa, these are CoCo's guests. I'm sorry, what are your names again?"

"Not a problem. I'm Genesis, and this is my man, Deuce."

Once Talisa stepped forward to say hello to them, the bodyguard was no longer blocking his view and Genesis could get a look at Arnez's woman. He was infuriated when he grasped that the woman he was determined to get belonged to Arnez.

"Hello," Talisa greeted them warmly, giving no indication that she had chatted it up with Genesis less than twenty minutes ago. In the mist of that, Genesis peeped Arnez's bodyguard whispering in his ear again.

"Baby, I'll be right back," Arnez told Talisa. "CoCo, keep my woman company while I go speak to someone briefly."

"I got you. I need to pick the brain of the woman who locked you down anyway. Talisa, would you like some champagne?"

"Sure."

"Come have a seat. I'll pour it for you."

Talisa sat down next to Genesis, welcoming his invitation. "So that's your man. I guess that means your off limits."

"I guess so."

"You don't sound so sure about that. Be honest, because if there is even this much of a chance," Genesis made a small space between his thumb and index finger, "That you could be mine, I'm taking it."

As Genesis picked up the champagne glass to hand Talisa, he caught a reflection of a red dot scanning in the direction of their table. "Oh, shit! Everybody get down!" Genesis yelled out, throwing his body on top of Talisa as a bullet barely missed her chest.

Deuce fell to the floor and reached over to make sure the lady he was kicking it with was okay, and damn near freaked out when he saw blood oozing from her neck. The bullet that missed Talisa had penetrated the woman behind her, killing her instantly.

Both Genesis and Deuce felt helpless, as neither was packing.

Just then, Genesis watched as Chanel crawled from up under the table, pulled two joints out her purse and started blasting. She was handling those guns like she was a professional hit-woman. At that moment, it was crystal clear to Genesis what role Chanel played in the operation and why CoCo kept her glued to her pocket. The riddle of bullets that the two men dressed in all black were beating upon the crowd came to a halt in less than twenty seconds after Chanel meticulously executed shots at both of them. The men appeared injured, but were still able to break out.

"CoCo, you straight?" Was the only thing Chanel wanted to know.

"I'm good. Girl, I'm so glad you my sister and that you were here."

By this time the whole club was going bananas. The crowd was damn near stampeding over each trying to get the hell out.

"Come on y'all, let's go out this back door," CoCo directed.

Genesis grabbed Talisa's arm and they all followed CoCo's lead. She knew exactly where she was going, and only a handful of other people did too, since there was no traffic going out that exit.

They all walked around towards the front of the club

and CoCo noticed the Rolls Royce parked across the street. "The car is over there." They all sprinted to the Limo, and once inside everybody just let out a deep breath.

"Talisa, are you okay?" Genesis held her closely trying to get her body to stop shaking.

Talisa buried her head in his neck still in shock. "That bullet missed me by inches! If it wasn't for you I would be dead!"

"But you're not. It's okay."

"Yo, the bullet that missed homegirl right there," Deuce pointed to Talisa, "Hit the chick I was chilling with—she's dead."

After Deuce revealed that information, Talisa started shaking even harder.

"CoCo, was those dudes after you? Because them cats seemed to be aiming directly at our table," Genesis wanted to know.

"I don't know. They might've been. See, that's why I like to keep my dealings low key. When motherfuckers out in these streets know you get real money, it's like a murder sign becomes emblazoned on your head. I don't even understand how them niggas got in the club with them type of weapons."

"The same way your sister did."

"But those are .44 magnums. You can sneak that in an oversized purse. You can't sneak no infrared beam type shit in the front door of a club without motherfuckers noticing. That was an inside job. Somebody let them niggas in knowing they were trying to shut shit down."

"Yo, Chanel, where the fuck you learn to handle heat like that? Yo quiet ass rose up from that table like Angelina

Jolie in 'Mr. & Mrs. Smith'," Deuce said, getting hyped.

"Oh, you didn't know? My sister is the baddest bitch on any coast. You think I keep her around me because we look alike? Nah, she can handle any weapon better than most men. Her game is serious. Our father taught her well."

Chanel didn't respond verbally to the praise her sister bestowed upon her. She just winked her eye.

"Your father? Let me find out y'all gotta family operation going on. But whatever works for you." Deuce decided to leave it alone.

"Whose phone is that ringing?" Genesis asked, still cradling Talisa in his arms.

"Oh, I think it's mine."

Genesis grabbed Talisa's purse off the floor and handed it to her. She pulled out her cell and answered, "Hello."

"Baby, where are you, are you okay?"

"I'm fine, Arnez. I left out with CoCo and her friends. We're in the car. What the hell happened in there?"

"I don't know. Come meet me in the front so we can go home."

"I don't want to go anywhere near that club. I'm going to stay at a hotel tonight. I'll call you in the morning."

"Talisa, I don't want you staying at a hotel. You need to come home with me, now."

"Arnez, please don't do this. I have the worse fuckin' headache and I don't feel like arguing with you. I'll call you in the morning." Talisa hung up her phone and Arnez called her right back. She didn't answer, and after he called for the fourth time she turned her cell off.

"Are you guys ready to get out of here?" Genesis wanted to get Talisa somewhere where she would feel safe.

"Yeah, we can go. But Talisa, are you sure you don't want to meet up with Arnez? I know he has to be worried about you."

"CoCo, I understand your concern for Arnez but right now I'm more concerned for myself. I want to go to a hotel so I can get me some sleep."

"You can stay at hotel we're at. We have two rooms. I'll sleep in the room with Deuce and you can have my room."

"Are you sure? I don't want to inconvenience you."

"I'm positive. I want you to get some rest too."

"Thank you," Talisa said, and leaned her head back on Genesis's shoulder as the car drove off.

CoCo sat back shaking her head as she studied Talisa and Genesis. She had been around the block enough times to know when chemistry was brewing between a woman and man. The closer she looked, the more it became clear to her that a love connection was erupting right in front of her eyes. If it was only about them and she didn't know the other player involved, she would toast to their future. But CoCo was all too familiar with Arnez and how territorial he was. In all the years she'd known him, he had never introduced her to any woman as his girlfriend, so she knew Talisa must be special to him. With that being the case, the same way Arnez held on tightly to business ventures he obsessed over, he would no doubt be the same, or even worse, with a woman that won his heart. CoCo prayed for Talisa and Genesis's sakes that after tonight they would go back to their normal lives, and that meant not having each other in it.

Chapter Five
Stay With Me

When the Limo pulled up in front of the Four Seasons Hotel, Talisa had already fallen asleep. Genesis didn't want to wake her because she seemed as content as a newborn baby wrapped in her mother's arms. He still couldn't believe that in less than twenty four hours he went from imagining what it would be like to know her at the airport to now holding her in his arms in front of his hotel. "Talisa, were here," he said softly in her ear.

"Oh, I got so comfortable I forgot where I was."

"No problem. Get your purse. I'll take you up to the room. And CoCo, I'll hit you up tomorrow so we can handle that."

Deuce got out first, and Genesis held the door open so Talisa could get out.

"By the way, Talisa, don't forget to call Arnez. I'm sure he'll be waiting to hear from you," CoCo reminded her.

Talisa seemed to ignore CoCo's comment and let the door shut behind her. CoCo was tempted to call Arnez and let him know Talisa's whereabouts, but knew that it would only cause problems for Genesis. And since they were doing business together she didn't want to bring drama in his path.

"You worried about the two of them aren't you?" Chanel asked, reading her sister's mind.

"And I have reason to be. Did you catch how they were looking at each other? I noticed that shit in the club but let it slide. Now Genesis un' saved that chick's life and they're going into a hotel together. This seems like some shit straight out of a romance movie. But this ain't Hollywood and those motherfuckers ain't acting."

"So what you gon' do?"

"What the fuck can I do? They grown. Hopefully Talisa values her life and Genesis will come to the conclusion that fucking with her would be more trouble than what it's worth. I'm staying out the shit. I have a lot of love for Arnez, but one thing I've learned is that when it comes to relationships of the heart, the messenger is the one that always catches it hard. Shit, that's Arnez calling me now." CoCo held up her phone showing Chanel his name on the screen.

"You not gonna answer it?"

"And tell him what? That I just dropped off his woman at the hotel with the guy I'm about to make some serious paper with? I think not. Chanel, I don't even have to school you on how the game go. We all out here trying to get the same thing—money. I ain't about to let some pussy get in the way of that. Arnez will try to shut down my dealings with Genesis before they even have a chance to begin if he thinks he's breathing in his girl's direction. Where would that leave me? He ain't gonna step in and lace my pockets with that paper. If anything, he'll probably blame me for having Genesis around his girl. Nah, I'm keeping my hands clean on this one. The only person I'm loyal to is you. That's because we got the same blood, and if I go down, you go down too. But everybody else, it's strictly business."

"I feel you. That's real talk. You see how I handled them motherfuckers in that club tonight? I wasn't about to let that shit go down."

"Yeah, you did your thing, ma. I held my tongue around Genesis and Deuce, but that shit got me bothered. I believe them shooters were aiming specifically for me. And whoever let them in knew that, so they co-signed. I need to know who was in charge of door security. I know it was Arnez's party, but I doubt he has a clue who was handling that. That's something the club would take care of. I don't want to go around asking too many questions and bring unnecessary heat on me or let the person or people behind it know that I'm hip to what's going on."

"That's smart."

"Umm hum, they should've prayed that I got taken out on the first try, because when I get to the bottom of this bullshit there's going to be a lot of slow singing and flower bringing."

****

When Genesis and Talisa entered his suite, he was relieved that he put in a late night request for the maid to clean his room before leaving for the club. He had done it originally because he figured he would meet some young lady at the party and bring her back to the hotel and twist her out, but making a good impression on Talisa far exceeded that.

"I'm gonna get a few of my things and then head over to Deuce's room. Do you need anything before I go?"

"Do you have to leave? Honestly, I don't want to be alone. I felt so secure when you held me in the car and I need for you to let me fall asleep in your arms."

Genesis stared at Talisa, not saying a word.

"Forget it. I guess you're thinking I should've gone home with Arnez because it's not your responsibility to take care of me. I understand. I'll try to be gone first thing in the morning." Talisa started messing with the blanket and pillows on the bed, feeling stupid for asking Genesis to stay with her and taking his silence as rejection.

"I would love to stay with you."

"You mean that? But you were speechless when I asked you."

"Being surprised by something does that to me. There's no place I would rather be than holding you as you fall asleep. That's the truth."

"I appreciate you saying that. Do you have a T-shirt I can sleep in?"

"Yeah."

"Thanks. I'm going to take a shower so you can leave it in the bathroom."

Talisa let the hot water drench her body as she tried to figure out what she was doing. Arnez was her boyfriend, but yet she was falling for another man that she barely knew, but being with Genesis felt so right to her. With him there wasn't this sense of pressure. That was in contrast to how she felt being with Arnez.

Talisa reminisced about the first day she met Arnez. She was leaving the campus at NYU after finishing one of her classes. She was rushing across the street trying to get to the cleaners before they closed because she was going to a party later that night and wanted to wear her favorite red dress.

When she got to the middle of the street she noticed a SUV zooming towards her, trying to catch the light before it turned red. All she remembered hearing was this loud screeching noise as the driver pushed down on his breaks. She began apologizing profusely because the signal said "Do Not Walk in" big ass white letters, which she ignored. But the driver was a complete gentleman. He pulled his car over to the side of the block to make sure she was okay.

"A pretty young lady like you has to be more careful. If I wasn't paying attention I could've ran you over."

"I know. I'm in a rush and I wasn't thinking straight."

"Where are you going? I can give you a ride."

"Thanks, but no thanks. You're a stranger. I don't even know your name."

"My name is Arnez Douglas. It's a pleasure to meet you." He extended his hand and Talisa couldn't help but be blinded by the huge, flawless diamond ring adorning his pinky finger. "And your name is?"

"Talisa Washington."

"So now can I give you that ride?"

"I don't think so. I really have to be going. The cleaners is going to be closing any minute. Again, sorry for the mishap."

Talisa turned and sprinted down the block, but Arnez wasn't going to let her get away that easily. He got in his SUV and slowly drove down the block she was on until he saw her banging on the front door of the cleaners. He rolled down the passenger window and blew his horn, determined to get Talisa's attention.

"I guess they're closed," Arnez said, stating the obvious.

"They literally closed five minutes ago. Somebody has to still be there."

"Let's make a deal. If I can get them to open the door and give you your clothes, you'll go out to dinner with me tonight."

"How in the hell are you going to do that?"

"That's not your concern. Do we have a deal or not?"

"I can't go out to dinner with you tonight. I'm going to a party."

"I won't take more than an hour of your time. We'll have a quick bite and then I'll drop you off at your party. If you don't enjoy my company then we can go our separate ways and call it a done deal. What do you say?"

"Fine, but I'm only agreeing because I'm curious as to how you're going to get my clothes."

Arnez put on his hazard lights and stepped out his truck. "You stay here, I'll be right back." He disappeared into the convenient store adjoining the cleaners and then came out five minutes later smiling.

"So what happened?" Talisa then heard the familiar bell ringing and turned her head to see the door to the cleaners opening. She threw her hands up in confusion. "What did you do?"

"Get your clothes and I'll tell you about it over dinner."

That night, Talisa did enjoy her dinner with Arnez, but no matter how many times she asked, he wouldn't reveal how he got someone to open the front door to the cleaners. After going out on a few more dates, it became clear to Talisa that that was how Arnez operated. He never wanted her or anyone else to know how he got things done, whether big or small. He got off on having a shroud of mystery surrounding him, and everyone around him trying to figure out his moves. It was also another way of Arnez keeping control of all situations. If he was the only one that had the inside blueprint on getting something done, no one stood a chance of beating him to the punch.

At first the tenacity in Arnez's personality drew Talisa in, but over time it was starting to become a turn-off. Because she lived in New York and he spent the majority of his time in Atlanta, it took a while for her to get a complete inside view of some of his less than stellar traits. But with school being out and spending a great deal more time with him, the last couple of months were a real eye opener. Every move he made seemed to be a game to him, and the people and things in his life were like possessions he used in his games. More and more Talisa was becoming fed up with being another prize he had added to his collection.

Enough about Arnez. If only for this one night I want

to fall asleep not worrying about what Arnez wants or how he would feel, Talisa said to herself as she dried off.

She put on the wife beater Genesis left in the bathroom for her, and part of her wished that he was her man.

When she came out the bathroom, Genesis was already in the bed and looked to be sleep. She observed him for a moment, studying his chiseled bone structure and caramel skin that looked as if it would melt on your fingertip with the slightest touch. After, Talisa turned off the light on the nightstand and laid beside Genesis. He reached over and wrapped his arm around her waist as if he'd been waiting to invite her in.

****

"Hello," CoCo answered halfway sleep.

"I've been calling you all night. Where is Talisa at?"

"Arnez, is that you?" CoCo knew he would be the only person calling her looking for Talisa, but she needed the extra time to get her lie situated in her head. She regretted even answering the phone, but because he caught her off-guard and she wasn't fully alert, her natural instant was to answer her cell. Normally, any call this early in the morning pertained to business.

"Of course it's me. Now where is Talisa? Did she spend the night with you?"

"No, she said she was getting a room."

"So what hotel is she at?"

"I don't have a clue. The driver dropped me and Chanel

off first and then took her wherever she wanted to go."

"Well give me the number to the driver. I'll call him."

CoCo had to sit up in bed and concentrate on her word usage because Arnez was on his game. "Damn, Arnez! I don't have that information. I don't even have a clue what car service that was because some people I was rolling with got the Limo. I was merely a passenger. I'm sure Talisa will be calling you soon. She's probably sleep. Don't stress yourself. But um... on another note, what happened at your party? It's like a war broke out in there."

"Who you telling? I got my people on it. Whoever's responsible for that bullshit ruined my fuckin' birthday party, and they will pay."

"Well, if you find out anything let me know."

"No doubt."

CoCo decided to call Genesis and wake him up to discuss business, hoping it would speed up the process of getting Talisa out of his hotel room. CoCo had to call his phone three different times before he finally answered.

"Yo," Genesis answered, looking at the clock to see what time it was.

"Genesis, it's nine o'clock. You need to get up so we handle the rest of our business."

"I thought we weren't meeting up until this afternoon."

"Some shit changed up at the last minute and we need to handle this earlier than originally planned."

"So what time you looking at?

"Now. I can meet you in front of the hotel in an hour."

"Damn, that soon?" Genesis looked over his shoulder and Talisa was sleeping so peacefully. "I need two."

"Two what?"

"Two hours."

"Alright, I'll see you at eleven." When CoCo hung up the phone she knew the reason Genesis needed more time was because Talisa was lying right beside him. "That nigga do not know what he is getting himself into," CoCo said, shaking her head.

****

Genesis's dick was rock hard staring at Talisa's body while she slept. The thin material of the wife beater was exposing her perfectly round breasts and erect nipples. Her succulent thighs were spread slightly apart, and Genesis wanted to slide his hand up her smooth skin and enter her sugar walls, but knew he had no right. Instead he got out of bed and took a cold shower.

After getting dressed he went next door to Deuce's room to wake him up.

When Deuce answered he was still in his boxer shorts, rubbing his eyes. "Man, what you doing over here so early? You supposed to be snuggled up with Miss High Class."

"CoCo woke me up saying that we needed to meet earlier. So get dressed. She'll be here in an hour."

"That's cool. But let's get to the good shit. Don't think I forgot you were supposed to stay in my room last night. But yo' slick ass never came back. So how did it go? Was the pussy as good as you imagined or was it overrated?"

"Deuce, two things: First, nothing went down between me and Talisa last night. She didn't want to be alone so

I stayed with her. Two, when and if I take it to that level with her, I won't be discussing it with you. You've used up your one time to ask me some disrespectful shit about her because you've been warned."

"A'ight, I get the message. You feeling homegirl and she's off limits. 'Nuff said."

"Cool. I'll see you downstairs at eleven."

When Genesis got back to his room, Talisa was still sleep. He decided not to wake her up and ordered room service. He sat in the chair by the window watching Talisa sleep while he waited for his breakfast. It seemed like yesterday he walked out of the juvenile detention facility, and now eight years later he was chilling in the Four Seasons Hotel with the most exquisite woman lying in his bed.

****

When Genesis turned eighteen and got released from the joint, he had no idea what would become of him. He returned to Philly with no family to go home to. He hadn't heard from his mother in years and didn't know if she and his sister were dead or alive. His father's side of the family didn't want anything to do with him and his grandmother on his mother's side hadn't heard from her daughter either. It was as if she disappeared without a trace.

For the first few months after Genesis came home his grandmother let him live with her, but soon he grew annoyed with the arrangement. Even though Genesis was extremely intelligent and got his high school diploma while locked down, he couldn't find a decent job. Now that he was out and away from the bad influences while in juvenile detention, part of him wanted to take some college courses and work towards getting a Bachelors Degree. But his grandmother wasn't having it. She demanded he get a job and help with the household bills if he wanted to live under her roof. He eventually landed a job doing some construction work, and for the next couple of years he worked a few different gigs but hated the long hours with minimum pay.

One afternoon while on a lunch break he ran into his childhood friend, Deuce. He convinced him, which wasn't hard to do under the circumstances, to leave that job making peanuts and come hustle with him on the streets. A few weeks later he moved out of his grandmother's house and shacked up with Deuce.

For Deuce, hustling on the streets was an easy way to afford nice clothes, a semi-fly whip, trick on pussy, pay some bills and keep money in his pockets. His ambition in the game never exceeded that. But for Genesis it was an opportunity to live another life. His goal was to take over and dominate the streets of Philly.

Deuce would just laugh every time Genesis would express those dreams. He didn't understand why Genesis felt the need to achieve so much. But being left alone with no mother, no father and never knowing his sister made Genesis feel that he had something to prove. He wanted everyone that abandoned him or told him he would never have shit to regret turning their backs on him. So while most of the young hustler's in the streets were either at the mall, running up in pussy or flossing in the club, Genesis stayed on the block trying to stack paper. It was difficult to make his mark because the game had cliques, which kept him on the low-level of the playing field. After many years of taking a few loses and having to start all over from scratch, Genesis had found his flow and was on his way to making some real coins; that was until the robbing crew made him their next target. But in the end it all worked out, and now he was closer than ever to being one of Philly's untouchables.

Chapter Six

Dangerous Attraction

Genesis checked his Audemars Piquet watch and realized it was time for him to meet CoCo. Talisa hadn't yet awoken from her deep sleep so he wrote her a quick note with his phone number on it. After grabbing his wallet and heading to the door, he paused and walked back over to the bed. He couldn't resist placing a gentle kiss on her lips before leaving.

****

When Deuce came out the lobby, he couldn't believe he was the first one there. Normally Genesis was early for all business dealings. *Damn, that chick must got him open*, he thought to himself.

A few seconds later he noticed Chanel pulling up in a navy blue Range Rover with CoCo in the passenger side. CoCo rolled her window down, and the first thing she said was, "Where's Genesis? He isn't with you?"

"He'll be down in a minute."

"Is he up there with Talisa?"

"Damn, ma, you just came right out with it. I don't be following dude's movements like that. You gonna have to ask him."

"I'll take that as a 'yes' then."

"You can take it however you like. But shit, it ain't my pussy and it ain't yours, so why you even give a fuck?"

"Because we got business to take care of and I don't like waiting."

"Then take yo' ass upstairs and get him. He in room 1106. But it'll be a waste because by the time you get there he'll be down here. So fall back and relax. It's only 11:05."

CoCo rolled her eyes and he peeped Chanel giving him a dirty look.

"My fault," he said, raising his hands up and continued jokingly, "I don't want to piss off the treacherous twins. CoCo, please don't sick Chanel on me. I saw firsthand how she handles her business."

"Whatever, nigga. Ain't nobody thinking about you. I do know Genesis need to hurry up."

"Here he comes now." Chanel was the first one to see him coming out the door.

"It's about time!" CoCo snapped.

"My fault. I lost track of time."

"Yeah, that's what happens when you sniffing after pussy."

"Yo, CoCo, you outta line with that. We here to do some business, so stay clear of my personal dealings. That means keep those salty comments to yourself."

"Ain't nothing salty about it. But that is my man's girl and I don't want to get caught in the middle of no drama. As a matter of fact, I'm trying to look out for your best interest."

"I'm good. But the less questions you ask, the less you know. That's how you keep yourself from being caught in the middle."

"I hear you. But because I believe we can make a lot of money together I'm going to give you fair warning. Arnez is not to be fucked with. So I don't care how pretty the face or tempting the pussy, no bitch is worth your life, and that's what your playing with if you get caught up with Talisa. So don't say I didn't tell you from jump. Now I'm done."

If CoCo was trying to aggravate Genesis she had accomplished it, but what she didn't accomplish was placing enough fear in him to stay away from Talisa. No matter what obstacles and hardships Genesis had been through in life, he believed he could get whatever he desired if he was willing to put in the work. And when it came to Talisa, he had already made up his mind that she was worth the work.

"I appreciate the warning, CoCo. I'll keep it close to my heart."

CoCo couldn't tell if he was being serious or sarcastic, but opted to let it go. "Good. Now ya ready to go?"

"Yep, the valet is pulling the car around now. We'll

follow you to the spot. Let's go, Deuce."

"Yo, homegirl is a trip," Deuce said once they were out of listening distance. "She act like Arnez is some brutal top five most wanted list type nigga."

"I don't give a fuck if he is. That nigga bleed just like you and me. His time move at the same pace as mine, so it is what it is."

"You right about that, but I know you're feeling Talisa, and if homeboy is a little psycho then maybe you need to back off."

"If I back off, it won't be because of Arnez, it'll be because that's what Talisa wants. Man, I'm just going with the flow. I'm going to follow her lead."

****

Talisa slowly started coming out of her sleep, and the first thing she did was slide her hand to the space beside her searching for the warmth of Genesis, but all she felt was emptiness. She opened her eyes for any indication of his body and was disappointed when he wasn't there.

"Damn, it's twelve-thirty! I can't believe I've been sleep this long," she said, looking at the clock.

Right when she was about to step out of bed and go to the bathroom, she heard someone knocking at the door. "Oh shit! That must be the cleaning lady. Can you please come back later?" she yelled, not feeling like answering the door. But the knocking continued.

She must don't understand English. I'm going to have to try some sign language. As Talisa headed to the door, the knock persisted. "Damn I'm coming!" Talisa barked, opening the door. Her heart dropped when she saw who was standing in front of her.

"Aren't you going to let me in?"

"Arnez, what are you doing here?"

"To get you, of course. I've been calling you all morning and your phone was turned off. Why is that?" Arnez brushed past Talisa, immediately sizing up the room and searching for any clue that sex had taken place.

"I turned my phone off before I went to sleep. I just woke up. I was about to call you," she lied.

"Now I'm here, so get dressed. We're leaving."

Talisa hesitated but knew it was in her best interest not to cause a confrontation. "Just give me a minute."

"I don't have a minute." Arnez grabbed the dress she was wearing last night off the couch and tossed it at Talisa, "Now get dressed."

Talisa held the dress in her hands and headed to the bathroom.

"Put it on, right here," Arnez said, pointing to the spot she had been standing in."

Talisa slipped out of the wifebeater and put on her dress. Before she had a chance to put on her shoes, Arnez had the door open ready to go. "Hold on, let me get my purse." As she picked up her purse, a piece of paper with scribbled writing and a phone number on it caught her eye. Instead of drawing attention to herself by reading it she slid it in her purse.

"Talisa, hurry up!" Arnez stated with fury dripping from his voice.

Arnez was mute from the elevator ride down and throughout the drive to his home. When they entered the gated community of Sugarloaf Country Club in Duluth, Talisa became nauseated. The sense of being imprisoned came over her. She wanted to jump out of the moving vehicle and run, but to where was the question.

Arnez continued his silence as he parked his silver Ferrari. Talisa took her time following him into the European hard coat stucco estate. When they entered the foyer, instead of trailing behind as he walked towards the formal living room, Talisa headed up the spiral staircase.

"Where do you think you're going?" Arnez stopped and asked when he realized Talisa wasn't behind him.

"Upstairs to take a shower."

"I need to speak to you."

"You had more than enough time to speak to me on our drive here. It was your decision not to utilize it."

"I was upset and didn't want to say something I would regret in anger."

"Oh, so what, just like that you're now over the anger?"

"No, I'm still angry but I have it under control now and I'm ready to talk."

"How can I forget? Arnez always has to be in control. Forget how other people feel, it's all about what *you* feel. Maybe now I'm angry and I don't want to talk to you!" Talisa said ending the conversation and walking up the stairs.

I'm so fucking tired of this nigga thinking it's all about him. Don't nobody give a fuck if he's angry. Shit, I almost got killed last night at his club and he only concerned about his anger, Talisa thought.

She stripped out of the dress she had worn last night and entered the spacious bathroom. She stepped in the steam shower ready to wash away the distaste Arnez left her with. But other thoughts engulfed Talisa's mind, like how good Genesis felt holding her as she slept. He had this hard exterior but he treated and exuded a warmth and gentleness that made him like a magnet.

Maybe it's time I moved on and stop fucking around with Arnez. Things aren't clicking with us and something about Genesis has me intrigued. Yeah, I need to have a serious talk with Arnez and let him know shit isn't working.

"What the fuck!" Talisa screamed as she was shaken out of thoughts.

"You think I'ma let you start disrespecting me in my own home?" Arnez barked as he dragged Talisa out of the shower by her wet hair.

Her body thumped on the marble tile floor causing her to feel as if her spine had broken in half. "Arnez, have you lost your mind!?"

"No, you've lost your fuckin' mind and I'm giving you one chance to get it back."

Talisa's heart was racing. She knew Arnez had a temper but never had he put his hands on her. Raised his voice, yes, but never this. She didn't know how to respond to his brutal behavior.

"When I say I want to talk, then you fuckin' listen," Arnez spit, tossing Talisa's naked body on the bed, pinning her down. "Don't you ever walk away from me when I'm speaking to you." Arnez saw the fear in Talisa's eyes and he ate it up. It gave him even more motivation to strike terror in her heart.

"First, you leave my muthafuckin' party with somebody else, and then I find you in another nigga's hotel room with his shit on. You lucky I don't kill yo' ass," he threatened, wrapping his hand around her throat. "You my bitch and betta not 'eva forget it, do you understand me?"

Talisa couldn't respond because the grasp Arnez had on her neck had her immobilized. She swung her legs in an attempt to communicate, as her face started turning color due to being cut off from all air supply.

Arnez eased up his grip. "Do you understand me?" he repeated, demanding an answer.

"Yes!" Talisa mouthed, paralyzed in fear.

"Good, because next time I'm not letting go of your neck; I'm crushing that shit!"

****

"Damn, we all the way out here in the middle of no-fucking-where!" Deuce commented as they pulled up to a warehouse in the outskirts of Atlanta.

"I told you this shit was far. Why you acting so surprised?"

"Saying something and seeing it for yourself is two different things. I hope Antwon will be able to find this place. I can't see this shit showing up on a GPS system."

"You always on some over exaggeration shit. This is what Antwon do. He'll be able to find the spot."

Right after Genesis said that, both the men saw Antwon

drive up in his nondescript mini van.

"That nigga kill me with all the college memorabilia shit, knowing he ain't seen the inside of a classroom since eighth grade," Deuce said.

"Deuce, man, that shit work. He be riding up and down these highways and cops don't fuck wit' him. They see all the stickers, tags and think he some college boy. Little do they know he rolling in a van full of enough narcotics to shut the whole city down."

"Yeah, and them electronic operated secret compartments don't hurt neither," Deuce noted.

"No doubt...oh shit, Chanel 'bout to blast my man, Antwon," Genesis chuckled when he noticed Chanel hopping out the Range Rover armed with her heat.

"Yo, that's a ballsy bitch right there," Deuce said, opening his car door.

"Chanel, chill! That's my people!" Genesis yelled out the window.

"How was she supposed to know?" CoCo responded as she stood in front of their ride. "The two of you so busy sitting in the car, you not letting us know who this stranger is pulling up on us. After the shit that went down last night, you know we busting ass first and taking names later."

"I feel you, ma, but I did tell you yesterday that my people was meeting us so he could get the shit. But I guess you forgot."

"No, I didn't forget. But without no name and vehicle description how was I supposed to know he was your people?" she responded, pointing in Antwon's direction, who was still sitting in his van as if waiting for a sign that the coast was clear.

"Come on now, CoCo, ain't nobody randomly falling up on this spot. If a car pull up in here, they know what the fuck is up."

"Deuce, I don't take shit for granted. This game is full of scandalous motherfuckers who will do anything for a come up. Somebody could be setting us up to rob and kill our asses. You never know."

"You right, CoCo. I shoulda been more clear about who was coming. Communication is key and it won't happen again. Now let's go handle our business."

CoCo nodded her head in agreement and headed to the entrance of the warehouse. Genesis and Deuce went in the opposite direction towards the car Antwon was occupying.

"Why you always pacifying that chick?" Deuce frowned to Genesis.

"Because we conducting business and I'ma treat her as such."

"Please! She so quick to get anal as fuck."

"Deuce, you beefing 'cause you can't get over the fact we doing major business with a female. Get over it. As long as CoCo can deliver on the product, then I'ma treat her with the same respect I treat anybody I'm doing business with and you need to do the same."

"I hear you, but I still think you baby her evil ass too much."

"For the amount of drugs we copping, you can call it whatever the fuck you like."

"Is everything straight?" Antwon questioned, getting out as Genesis and Deuce got to his van.

"Yeah, we straight. Homegirl was just PMS-ing," Deuce popped. Genesis glared in his direction letting him know to let the petty bullshit go.

"Yo, when I saw that chick coming at me with her heat I thought it was about to be a shootout in this motherfucker. I said to myself, that sexy piece of ass is fine as hell, but she will get got if that weapon don't disappear."

"Exactly!" Deuce said, giving Antwon a pound.

"Listen, we had a minor misunderstanding but it's all good. You got the loot, right?"

"Of course. Always prepared."

"Cool. Now back up the ride so we can load this shit up and be out"

"I'm with you, Genesis. I'm ready to get the fuck outta Atlanta and take my black ass back to Philly. Tonya been blowing my phone up too. I need to get back to shorty."

"You can go back, but I was thinking about staying an extra day or so," Genesis told him.

"I bet you was. Homegirl got you going," Deuce said.

"What? You met a cutie up in the ATL?" Antwon inquired, nudging Genesis's arm.

"No comment."

"Yes the fuck he did. But he need to forget her since shorty is off limits," Deuce chimed in.

"What, she gotta man? That don't stop shit," Antwon said.

"My sentiments exactly, Antwon." Genesis eyed Deuce, knowing he would have some slick shit to say, and he did.

"If we believe what the dynamic duo over there said, then he ain't any man he is 'The Man'. And me, personally, don't think no woman, no matter how pretty the pussy, is worth some unnecessary drama. You feel me?"

"We ending this conversation now. Antwon, back the car

up and come on. Deuce, you know how the twins don't like to be kept waiting."

"We sure don't," CoCo said, standing a few feet away with her arms crossed. "Come check the product so we came wrap this shit up."

"I don't be agreeing with CoCo on shit, but we seeing eye to eye on the wrap this shit up thing," Deuce said, speeding up his walk and ready to break the fuck out.

The heroin and cocaine was packed up and placed on the long table, ready as soon as you stepped in the warehouse. It was a huge open space, but the only thing there were the drugs that Genesis was purchasing.

"I was expecting to see this place filled with drugs, guns and all sorts of illegal shit," Genesis said as he inspected the product.

"Nah, I always try to take extra precautions. With each new client and business transaction we use a different warehouse location. It minimizes the chances of someone setting us up. In this business it can still happen, but doing it this way just makes the opportunity much slimmer," CoCo explained.

"I like that because you never know who might snake you out in this game. All this shit is straight, so we gon' load up."

"Not yet."

"What is it now?" Deuce groaned, making it clear he was annoyed.

"I need to count that cheddar first," CoCo stated, eyeballing Deuce.

"Not a problem. Antwon, bring the money over here," Genesis directed.

Chanel met Antwon halfway, taking the duffel bag out of his grasp and handing it over to her sister. The three men sat on the edge of the van as the twins sifted through the cash, making sure it wasn't a dollar short.

"Them chicks ain't no joke. As fine as they are, I'd be scared to fuck wit' some broads like that," Antwon said quietly to Deuce and Genesis.

"Why?"

"Why? Genesis, I can't believe you would even ask why. They probably know more tricks than the three of us combined. You know what I'm spitting is the truth. I would always be sleeping with one eye open if I fucked around wit' one of those broads." All three of them laughed simultaneously at Antwon's comment.

"Sorry to interrupt your chit chatting, but we good. You can get your shit. I'm sure you all are anxious to get back to Philly."

"I know I am. So anxious that, Antwon, I'll help you pack this shit up." Deuce sprinted to the table and started grabbing packages.

"Genesis, let me have a word with you before we break out," CoCo said.

"Sure." Genesis followed CoCo outside the warehouse near her truck. "So what's up?"

"I'm hoping we can make a lot of money together and this deal is the first of many."

"I'm hoping for the same thing."

"So that dude, Antwon, is he the one that will always handle your pickups?"

"Unless I tell you otherwise, no doubt."

"Cool. I prefer as few people as possible know about

transactions."

"I agree. But CoCo, why don't you tell me what's really on your mind, because it ain't this."

"True."

"So spill, because at the rate them niggas loading that shit you ain't got but a few minutes to say whatever is on your mind."

"I only want to reiterate what I told you earlier; stay away from Talisa."

"And I'ma tell you the same thing I told you earlier; stay out of it."

"I know you a grown ass man and I'm not tryna boss you…seriously I'm not. I think you a cool individual not only on a business tip but as a person. This isn't about me just protecting my investment because I know we can make a lot of money together. I don't want to see anything happen to you."

"CoCo, I believe you're being up front with me, but ain't nothing going down between me and Talisa. But even if there was, I ain't worried about that nigga, Arnez."

"If you not worried about your safety, than worry about Talisa's. I don't know anything about her, but I know everything about Arnez. He is not gonna stand for a woman of his being sweet on no other nigga."

"Oh, so you think Talisa sweet on me!" he teased.

"This ain't a joke. I know the two of you are sweet on each other. All I'm saying is that if you care anything about that woman's welfare, back the fuck off. I've said enough and it looks as if your boys are done."

Genesis turned around and saw Deuce and Antwon shutting the doors. "Thanks, CoCo. It was a pleasure doing business with you."

"I hope you'll be calling for a re-up soon," she grinned, shaking Genesis's hand.

"So do I."

"If you decide to stay longer, give me a call. There is always something poppin' in the ATL."

"Will do, but there isn't anything left for me in Atlanta. It's time for me to go home to Philly."

"I agree."

Genesis had it bad for Talisa, but he knew CoCo was speaking real shit. It wasn't only about him. If Arnez was as treacherous as CoCo hinted, then he could fuck up Talisa's life by chasing her. He didn't want to bring that sort of chaos her way, especially if she wanted to be with dude. There was no question in Genesis's mind that the two of them had ridiculous chemistry, but it didn't give him a clear indication that Talisa was ready to bail on her man to be with him. And unless she let him know that, Genesis was putting Talisa out of his mind.

Chapter Seven
Success

"This our city! We run this shit! We ballin' motherfuckers!" Deuce yelled out from the 34th floor balcony of the high-rise condominium. Tonya and her two girlfriends giggled and clicked their champagne glasses together, cheering her man on.

"Man, chill out. You gon' have my neighbors complaining and shit," Genesis said, trying to calm Deuce down.

"Fuck your neighbors! The money you paid for this crib, we can all scream out butt ass naked with some bullhorns if that's what the fuck we wanna do."

"Deuce, chill. As far as everybody in this building is concerned I'm a hardworking, tax paying, law abiding, upstanding citizen. I don't need you fucking that up with no extra attention. Now chill!"

"A'ight, but damn, nigga, look at you. Who woulda

ever imagined that this is your life, chillin' in a bangin' ass luxury condo overlooking Center City? You got views of the river and parks I didn't even know existed in Philly. My man, you have truly fuckin' arrived."

Genesis stood on his balcony staring at the night time skyline view of Philadelphia, and although he was proud of all he had accomplished in such a short span of time, each day he was plotting on how to get an even bigger slice of the American dream. His stacks were stacked high, but he knew with the right moves they could become even higher.

After the initial deal with CoCo three months ago, he had re-upped eight times. He had no idea that shit would take off so fast. Part of it was because the dope they were supplying was top-of-the-line, and the other part was pure luck.

In those couple of days he was handling his business in Atlanta, the feds had come in and did a major sweep down. Damn near all the major niggas got locked up and the streets were dry. You couldn't get any decent drugs from anywhere, so when Genesis came home with his new product, motherfuckers thought it was Christmas and he was Santa Clause. Not only were the streets thirsty for his drugs, but he was able to up the price because the demand was crazy. The money was flowing like water from a faucet and the shit didn't ever seem to turn off. Within weeks, Genesis would be calling CoCo, needing more drugs. She was happy to comply but was stunned at the rate he was flipping that shit.

"Yeah, no doubt we fo' sho' stackin' paper, but there's a lot more money out there to make," Genesis finally said, coming out of his private silence.

Tonya's friend, Denise grinned at Genesis, loving his man-on-a-mission attitude. And Genesis wasn't blind to it. Like most women who knew his status in the game, they were practically cumming in their panties at the sheer thought of having a chance with him. But that shit didn't faze Genesis a bit. His first, second and third priority was making money. He viewed pussy as a necessity to let off stress, and that was pretty much it. He would never consider settling down with the sack chasers he came in contact with. But until he reached the financial level he wanted, he had no desire to tie himself down to any woman and simply enjoyed the company of party girls with pretty faces and phat asses.

"Genesis, am I staying with you tonight?" Denise asked, sipping seductively on her glass of champagne.

"No, he's staying with me," Monica barged in, brushing her well endowed ta-ta's against Genesis's chest. On any other day the two young women were the best of friends, sharing clothes, gossip and living quarters, but not tonight. Them ho's both had dollar signs in their eyes and Genesis was the moneymaker.

Genesis sized up both women. Denise was a petite sexy bunny with light brown short hair, accentuated by caramel and blond highlights that feathered around her face, and an extra long bubble fringe ending at the eyelashes, which emphasized her wide amber colored eyes.

Monica, on the other hand, was a silky brown stallion. She came a few inches below Genesis's six-foot two inch frame, and had long, endless legs with ass and tits that didn't quit. Both women had totally different looks, but was each holding their own in the beauty department. Genesis couldn't go wrong either way, but there was something about Monica he didn't like, and it was her aggressiveness. He knew both women were anxious to give up the pussy, but he preferred the more demure vibe of Denise to the forceful one from Monica.

"Ladies, both of you are exquisite. It's impossible for me to choose," Genesis said, stroking their egos so the one that was rejected won't take it too hard.

"Baby, I've already made the decision for you," Monica told Genesis, and then said to her girlfriend, "Denise, I'm sure Deuce and Tonya won't have a problem giving you a ride home."

Denise gritted her teeth ready to slap the shit out of her friend and roommate, but they had always made a pact that no man, no matter how fine or rich, would come between them. "Whatever you say, Monica."

"See, there! Denise don't have no problem with my decision. We good."

"I like that. Friends willing to compromise. But can you excuse me, ladies? I need to speak with Deuce for a moment."

"No problem, baby. I'll be here waiting," Monica said, licking her lips. "Girl, I hit the jackpot with that sexy ass nigga!" The girls slapped each other's hands.

"You know I'm jealous and shit. I made the first move then you came over here tossing your tits around interrupting me."

"Denise, you move too slowly on sealing the deal. I couldn't let a nigga that's fine and chipped slip through my fingers. But when he be hitting me off with that shopping spree money, you know I got you, boo."

"I'ma hold you to that shit, so don't forget," Denise said, no longer mad that her girlfriend would be the one living it up in luxury and not her.

Genesis made his way to the living room where Deuce and Tonya were sitting on the ivory bone colored sofa, making out as if they were at a drive-in movie.

"Umm, sorry to interrupt, but Tonya, I need to speak with Deuce." Deuce slapped her ample ass letting her know to get up.

"Okay. Deuce I'll be on the balcony," Tonya told him.

"Cool. We leaving in a few so get your shit together."

Tonya strutted off feeling like she was the luckiest chick in the world to have Deuce as her man.

"So what up partner?" Deuce said as Genesis sat down next to him on the sofa.

"You tell me. I think if I hadn't come in here the two of you would've started fuckin' right here in my living room."

"Nah, I wouldn't do that to you, homie, but it was tempting like a motherfucker. Tonya got some good pussy and her head game is sensational."

"Nigga, you crazy! But she doing something right because this the longest you un lasted wit' any broad. I thought for sure it woulda been a two week fuck fest then a trade-in for a newbie like it be with the rest of your women."

"Tonya's different. I think she a keeper."

"Good for you. Having a steady may calm you down and get you to focus more on making money."

"What is you talkin' 'bout? I makes plenty of money."

"I'm talkin' *real* money."

"Genesis, you know I respect your grind, but I don't

have to be living on some king type shit like you. When I got in the game I never even thought I would be making half of the money I'm gettin' now, so I'm good. But that's your problem. You work too damn much. Did you see them two bad bitches Tonya brought over here? And all you can think about is making mo' money."

"Speaking of those two, that's what I wanted to speak to you about."

"Oh shit! You want to fuck one of them, or both? Let me know and I'll gladly hook that shit up."

"I know you would. But I'm only interested in one."

"Which one?"

"Denise."

"Oh, the little cutie. Yeah, she sexy. Stay right here, I'll go get her."

"Wait. The problem is the girl Monica already put down her claim, so Denise backed off."

"That ain't a problem. Monica gotta step the fuck aside. I'll tell her it's time to go."

"But I don't want to cause no problems between the two of them. So don't cause no scene, be diplomatic with the shit."

"I got you. I'ma handle it real cool. I'll be right back."

Deuce wasted no time in setting the record straight with Monica. When he went to the balcony, the ladies were on another bottle of champagne, laughing and giggling like they were living the good life.

"Hey baby, you ready to go?" Tonya asked when Deuce walked up.

"Yeah, it's time to break out."

"Okay, cool. Monica is staying here with Genesis so we

gonna drop Denise home."

Monica was flashing her best beauty pageant smile while Denise was frowning, heated that she lost the prize, or so she thought.

"There's been a change of plans."

"What, we staying here tonight?" Tonya asked, sounding confused.

"No, we going to my crib, but Denise is staying here, not Monica."

The three women stared at each other in bewilderment. In their minds the deal had been sold, told and closed. Deuce was hitting them from left field and none of them were happy about it, except for Denise. Her frown magically turned into a smile.

I'm back in the game, Denise chanted on the inside.

"Deuce, maybe you're confused, because Monica is the one Genesis chose, not Denise," Tonya explained, wanting Monica to be the front-runner.

Tonya was biased anyway because she was closer to Monica. Although she kept her true feelings on the low, Tonya couldn't stand Denise. They had competed for the same man's attention on numerous occasions, and Denise always came out ahead. If Denise had been out with her the night she met Deuce, she figured he would've been another catch that got away. For reasons beyond her comprehension, she felt that men got suckered by the fake feminine innocence that Denise perpetrated. Tonya was going to do everything possible to make sure that didn't happen with Genesis.

"It ain't no maybe. Deuce you are confused," Monica stood up pointing her finger. "You need to go get Genesis right now. He'll set the record straight. I'm the one that's staying the night and Denise is going the fuck home."

Denise didn't utter a word. She sat modestly with her legs crossed as if a halo swirled over her head.

Genesis sat back on the sofa oblivious to the stage show taking place outside on his balcony. He was relieved he didn't have to break the news to Monica that she wasn't the winner, but instead the second runner up. As he closed his eyes beginning to relax, the commotion he was unaware of was bombarding its way into his space.

"Genesis, your man Deuce here is a tad bit confused. He rambling on about how you want Denise to stay here with you and I'm going home. I tried to hip him to the fact that he got the name and location switched backwards. Please clear this bullshit up so Tonya can go home with her man and take Denise with her." Monica stood confidently with her hand glued on her hip like everybody had it wrong but her.

"Where is Denise?" Genesis asked, seeing that she was the only one not bringing the noise.

"She sitting outside. She understands that Deuce made a mistake and ain't trippin' off of it," Tonya added, letting Monica know she had her back.

"Tonya, stay out this shit. Ain't no mistake been made. Genesis don't want Monica. He checkin' for Denise. Now get your shit so we can go," Deuce told her.

Genesis shook his head because the conflict he was trying to avoid was playing out right in front of his eyes. It was at that moment when Genesis gave no rebuttal to what Deuce said, and Tonya and Monica had to accept that once again, Denise won.

"Monica, you are a prime catch and any man would do

just about anything to have you on his arm," Genesis said trying to smooth things over.

"Then why didn't you pick me, Genesis? Hmm?"

"Because I know when we go out all the niggas will be checkin' for you and disrespecting me with their glares and stares. Bottom line, you too much woman for me and I wouldn't be able to handle my jealously over all those other men tryna get at you. With my life being hectic, I don't need any additional distractions."

"Yeah, right! Save that lying ass bullshit for Denise. I wish you two the best of luck, but I guarantee you missed out by not picking me. Come on Tonya, take me the fuck home!"

"I'll talk to you tomorrow," Deuce said, giving Genesis a devilish grin.

When Genesis heard the door close shut, he quickly went to bolt the locks, making sure all access was cut off.

"Is the coast clear?" Denise emerged from the balcony wearing nothing but her pink strapless stilettos, ecstatic the coin had tossed in her favor.

"Damn, that's what I call a re-introduction!"

"I call it showing my appreciation. Now are you going to come over here or do I need to come get you?"

"You stay yo' sexy ass right there, I'll come to you."

Genesis took his time nearing Denise. He was taking great pleasure in studying every inch of her body. Genesis had no idea she had all that going on under her clothes. In her halter dress, you could tell Denise had a cute figure, but it appeared tiny. In the flesh, her frame was petite but plump in all the areas that mattered most to a man.

"Now have a seat so I can give you a proper thank you,"

Denise said, gliding her body in his direction.

Genesis sat down on the sofa and slid his hands from the tip of her hardened nipples to the base of her firm ass, caressing every curve.

Denise knelt down, comfortably placing her knees on the chinchilla rug and unzipped Genesis's slacks and pulled down his gray boxer briefs, revealing the magnificent tool she imagined a fine thug-ass nigga like him would be working with. Without a misstep in her performance, she draped her luscious lips around Genesis's dick and got her head to bobbing as if she had been a hand-picked protégé of Superhead.

"Genesis, are you pleased with the choice you made?" Denise stopped to ask the question right at the point she felt his dick pulsating and ready to explode.

"Fuck yeah!" Genesis moaned, seizing the back of her hair.

"I knew you would be."

Denise continued her gratifying techniques that had Genesis open.

He briefly glanced out the dramatic curved glass on his floor-to-ceiling windows, then laid his head back and closed his eyes, savoring each wet stroke that had his dick rock hard. *I damn sure made the right choice! I may have to keep shorty around for a minute,* Genesis decided as he erupted in Denise's mouth.

****

Talisa cringed in repulsion as she lay on her back while Arnez pounded on her insides. All she could do to keep from crying was close her eyes until this act that was supposed to be called sex was over. She yearned for earplugs, because having to listen to the groans and moans Arnez emitted made his fucking that much more unbearable. In her wave of misery she pondered how in the fuck she went from an independent college student to an emotionally broken down punching bag.

After the first time Arnez dragged Talisa out of the shower and threatened to end her life, each day had been a downward spiral to pure hell. Arnez acted like he found the secret cure to dominate his woman and exploited it at every given chance in a bid to never surrender his control. With each new day, Talisa promised herself she would escape her doom, but fear had her paralyzed. She wanted to call her parents and beg for help, but each time she'd pick up the phone, shame and embarrassment would force her to hang up. Now she felt alone, helpless and at Arnez's mercy.

"Oh shiiiiiiiit, I'm 'bout to come!" he grumbled then grunted, releasing himself inside of Talisa. Sticking with consistency, Arnez rested his body firmly on top of her until he felt the last drop of his seed swim far up. "If we didn't make a baby after what I just dropped in you, we going to see a doctor," he said, rolling off her.

"Arnez, I don't think that's necessary."

"I've been up in you everyday for the last what few months and you ain't got pregnant yet. Something is wrong."

"I'm sure nothing is wrong. Sometimes getting pregnant takes time."

"Maybe you can't make no babies. If so, we need to find

that out."

"Why are you so pressed about getting me pregnant? I'm too young to have a baby right now anyway. I need to go back to school and get my degree."

"We already had this discussion. I told you I wanted a son and that you would sit out of college this semester and probably next."

"Unless you made a deal with the devil, there isn't a hundred percent certainty that I'll have a son. I could very easily have a daughter," Talisa said, knowing damn well if she had her way, she wouldn't be having either. Unbeknownst to Arnez, Talisa had taken precautions to make sure she didn't get knocked up by him. She had been faithfully swallowing a birth control pill daily behind his back.

"Don't concern yourself with the sex of the baby. All you need to concentrate on is getting pregnant," Arnez said, rubbing her stomach.

"Whatever makes you happy, baby."

"Now you talking right. See, if you practice keeping that attitude your life will be so much easier."

"I'm working on it."

"Don't work on it, do it."

"I will, but Arnez, I really need to go home and visit my parents."

"Why do you need to see them?"

"I have to tell them that I'm not going back to school this semester."

"The phone lines are working perfectly."

"I don't want to tell them over the phone, I want to see them in person."

"That's not an option I'm giving you."

"Why?"

"Because right now you're still fragile. If you go visit your parents they may influence you to stay in New York. Then I would have to come track you down, which would piss me off and things will get ugly. To avoid that you need to stay here."

"Doesn't it bother you that you basically have me living like a prisoner?"

"That isn't true. You're free to go and come as you please."

"How can you say that with a straight face? Every time I leave this house I have to be escorted by one of your hired goons. That isn't freedom."

"It's for your own protection."

"The only person I need protection from is you."

"You damn right!" Arnez reminded Talisa of that by landing a closed backhand slap. The burning sensation on Talisa's lower cheek let her know a bruise would be decorating her face shortly. "See what you made me do?" Arnez calmly put the blame on Talisa and got out of bed.

"Is this ever gonna stop?"

"It's up to you. If you act right and follow my rules the world is yours, remember that."

Talisa's bottom lip trembled as she wiped away the one tear that trickled down her cheek. *If only I could rewind time,* she thought before closing her eyes.

Chapter Eight
Man Down

When Denise pulled up to Philadelphia's premiere fine dining restaurant at 1523 Walnut Street, Monica and Tonya's mouths dropped.

"How in the fuck did you get Le Bec-Fin coins?" Monica smacked as the ladies got out of the car.

"From the same person who let me drive his Benz tonight," Denise boasted.

The ladies entered the restaurant that had the 19th century elegance of a Parisian dining salon, and were greeted by a tall, pencil thin hostess. "How may I help you?"

"Yes, I made a reservation for three under Denise Sanders."

The woman paused for a few moments as she located the name. "Yes, here you are. Would you ladies please follow me."

Denise led the pack with her head tilted high up in the air making it known she had just as much right to be in the exclusive establishment as the snooty white-collar crackers patronizing the place. Monica and Tonya didn't feel quite as confident.

"Here we are, ladies. Your waiter will be with you shortly."

"Thank you," Denise said, giving a fake Holly*weird* smile.

"You actin' mighty comfortable in here," Tonya commented as her eyes darted around.

"This is one of Genesis's favorite restaurants so we're frequent customers."

"You've been dating Genesis for maybe a couple of months now, and this dude letting you hold one of his whips, taking you to fancy places like this, and giving you enough money to treat your girls to this joint. What the fuck is going on? I been fucking Deuce for months now and we barely getting past TGI Friday's."

"Maybe the fucking isn't the problem, it's the sucking you need to work on," Denise joked with an undertone of seriousness.

Monica and Tonya locked eyes, and both were thinking the exact same thing. *This bitch gets on my nerves.*

"I don't think sucking is the problem. I ended up with a guy who doesn't have any interest with the finer things in life. But that's cool because he makes up for it in other ways," Tonya said, trying to defend her man.

"That's probably what it is, because my baby damn sure has a penchant for wanting the best. He spoils me without even trying. You see this bag I'm rockin'?" both women glanced at the crocodile clutch on the table. "I was at the

Gucci store with Genesis because he was buying some luggage. He didn't feel it was right for him to get something and I leave empty handed, so he got me this expensive ass purse. That's the type of shit my man do for me."

"Genesis your man now?" Monica pried.

"He might as well be."

"That ain't the question. Has dude stepped to you and claimed you as his woman?" Monica wanted the yes or no answer, not the rainbow version.

"No, but it's coming. Monica, don't front. I barely be home anymore because I'm laid up at that nigga's crib. Trust me, soon he'll be asking me to move in."

"I wouldn't count on that, Denise."

"May I get you ladies something to drink?" the waiter asked, interrupting the tongue lashing Denise was ready to put on Tonya.

"Yes, get me your most expensive bottle of French Chardonnay."

"As you wish. I'll be back shortly to take your order."

"I see you tryna show off, ordering some fancy wine like you a fuckin' socialite."

"Monica, please. I know you mad 'cause Genesis chose me, but get over it. Back to you, Tonya. Why shouldn't I count on having a serious relationship with Genesis?"

"It may turn into something serious, but from what Deuce say, all Genesis is focused on is business. He ain't really tryna be tied down to nobody."

"Maybe I'm changing that."

"You could be, but it's hard to teach an old dog new tricks."

"True, especially when you got one with three baby

mamas and no bigger ambition but to be hood rich," Denise sniped, taking a jab at Tonya.

"I knew there was a reason I couldn't stand your ass."

"Oh, besides the fact that the men you want always choose me?"

"See, you always been a stuck-up hoochie who thinks the sun rise and sets on your triflin' ass, but it don't. So you know, when God created pussy, he gave every damn woman one, not just yo' ass. So stop actin' like it's all about you, Denise. Now where is the waiter? I need to eat some damn food before I get us all thrown out for whipping yo' ass."

****

"I think you should make a right on the next street," CoCo suggested to Chuck as she sat in the passenger side of the Range Rover.

"What street is the club on?"

"You know where The Compound is, over on Brady Avenue," CoCo reminded him as she continued to text back and forth on her Blackberry.

"Damn, I went the wrong way! Let me turn around," Chuck said, doing a U-turn in the middle of the street. "Did Chanel say what time she was meeting you over there? I don't want to have her waiting too long by herself."

"No, and you know I hate going places without my sister. I mean you know I got love for you, Chuck, but when Chanel is with me I feel extra protected like I'm untouchable."

"You can feel that way with me too. Shit, I've known you and your sister since you were sassy little girls with pigtails. I ain't gonna let nothing happen to you and I put that on my life. Your father would turn over in his grave if I did."

"Chuck, do you ever think about my dad?"

"Everyday. Your father was a good man. They don't make em' like him anymore. He brought honor to the streets"

"Then why didn't he honor my mother and marry her?"

"I don't know."

"Yes you do. You worked for my father for over twenty years. You know damn near everything about him."

"I know that he loved you and your sister very much and he always said that if anything ever happened to him he wanted me to promise I would look out for the two of you. I've kept that promise, and will do so until the day I die."

"If he loved us so much, why wasn't he around more?"

"CoCo, why do you want to indulge in such a heavy conversation that's in the past?"

"Because the shit has always been on my mind, but every time I bring it up to you, you either change the subject or do what you doing now—avoid it. This shit ain't gon ever be in the past for me until I get answers."

"You want answers? Truth is your father was a street nigga to the core. The only emotional attachment he had was to money. He didn't want to marry your mother or any woman for that matter. But he was always upfront about that with every woman he dealt with."

"So you saying it was my mother's fault that she got knocked up by a man that didn't want her?"

"What I'm saying is your father did the only thing he

was capable of doing, and that was to financially support his kids and the mother of his children. He never made promises beyond that. And he was able to keep them even from his grave. Do you believe you and your sister would have the connections to be on the level you're at if it wasn't for your father?"

"I know a lot of the major players originally only fucked wit' us because we Chauncey Armstrong's daughters. But it's our work ethics that keep them coming back."

"I'm not trying to take nothing from how you handle your business. I know your father would be proud of both of you, but the point is, when he was alive he had your back and in death he does too. I know what the real problem is."

"What you mean? I told you the real problem."

"No, that's your excuse. In your mind you believe Chauncey didn't marry your mother because he didn't want the two of you. But that's simply not the case. When your mother went into labor your father dropped everything he was doing and rushed to the hospital so he could be there when you all were born. One day he confided in me that with all the money he had made in the streets, the two of you were his greatest accomplishments."

"He really said that?"

"Yes, he did. So don't ever think for one moment that he didn't want you or love you. He was just a complicated man, like so many men who marry the streets. Now, if I'm ever going to find this club I have to stop talking to you."

"I don't know why you don't use the navigation system."

"You know I'm old school. I don't mess with that shit.

I'll find it, just keep doing that text thing and let me be."

CoCo laughed at Chuck before lying back in the seat replaying what he had said. She wished that Chanel had been in the car to hear it because both of them had fucked up views of men because of the relationship with their father, or Chauncey which is what he had the twins call him. The word "dad" or "father" made Chauncey feel old, and he was constantly trying to defy aging. Chauncey Armstrong wasn't the typical parent. He never took the girls to the park or taught them how to ride a bike. He hardly ever came around until they turned nine or ten. He had no use for little girls. He felt you couldn't do anything with them except dress them up and give them dolls to play with.

As the girls got older, he decided that their gender wouldn't stop him from teaching them what he felt was important—learning a hustle. Chauncey's visits were few and far between, but when he did come around, instead of going to the movies he would teach them how to play cards and make money at it. And there was no hopscotch or jumping rope at his crib. Chauncey preferred the shooting range he had in the back of his house, and made the twins sit on the side and watch him practice.

CoCo never forgot on a rare occasion when Chauncey took them to the mall and a girl bumped into Chanel and didn't say excuse me. Chanel could've let it go, but she wouldn't. She ran behind the girl, and at the time Chanel was twelve and the girl was at least three or four years older than her. Chanel said in the same composed manner she uses now, "You bumped into me and didn't say excuse me."

The teenager frowned at Chanel, then looked at her friends and started laughing. "Little girl, get the fuck out my face before I show you what a real bump feel like," the teenager threatened, pointing her finger in Chanel's chest.

"Chauncey, come on, we have to go help Chanel. She about to get herself in some mess."

"No, we are going to stay right here. If your sister don't want to be a person to let shit go, then she gonna have to learn to back it up."

CoCo looked on from a few feet away, hoping Chanel would give up and walk away, but knowing how stubborn Chanel was, she highly doubted it.

"If you put your hands on me one more time, I'ma break your finger."

"Oh shit! Shorty got fire wit' her," the teenage girl's friends jeered.

Not to be shown up by some little girl, the teenager jabbed her finger into Chanel's forehead, chastising her.

Chanel kept her word, and latched onto the girl's finger tightly and began twisting it. The teenager made a mistake by underestimating Chanel's strength.

"I told you not to put your hands on me."

"Ouchhhhhh!" she screamed out in pain. Let me go!"

Chauncey and CoCo ran up and pulled Chanel off the girl.

"That little is girl crazy!" the girl's friends were blabbing amongst themselves as the teenager was squirming, still in pain.

"Chanel, are you alright?" CoCo asked, concerned about her sister.

"I'm fine. It's the other girl you need to be worried about."

"You listen here, Chanel. With all that anger brewing, yo'

shit gonna have to be tight. That fool over there might not have been no match for you, but trust they'll always be someone stronger or faster. With a mouth and temper like you got, you gon' have to back it up with more than your fists."

"What are you suggesting, Chauncey?" Chanel wanted to know.

"It's simple. No more sitting on the sidelines when I'm practicing my shooting. From now on, you'll be right there beside me, learning how to handle a weapon," Chauncey decided.

Just like that, Chanel went from keeping CoCo company on the sidelines, to becoming a student to the master. Her skills superseded even what Chauncey had in mind. Chanel more than learned how to handle a weapon; she became a beast at it.

Those were the few and rare moments shared with their father that made them feel close to him. Most of the time, it was as if they didn't exist to him. It didn't help the cause having a bitter mother who constantly reminded them of their father's absence. After all these years their mother still harbored resentment and never forgave Chauncey for not marrying her.

"We finally here," Chuck said, putting the truck in park.

"You're not gonna put the truck in valet?"

"Now you know I don't do valet. If some shit go down, I don't want to have to chase one of these knuckleheads down to get the keys."

"You always make that point, and I can't front, it's a valid one.

"You don't have to tell me. I already know. Do you see

Chanel or her car anywhere?" Chuck asked, as he scoped out the parking lot.

"Hold up, this Chanel calling me right now. Where you at?"

"I'm finishing some things now and I'm on my way. Did y'all get to the club yet?"

"Umm hmm, we got here a few minutes ago."

"Which room do you want me to meet you in?"

"Probably The Loft. Call me when you get here and I can tell you exactly where I am. How long do you think it'll be?"

"Give me thirty minutes."

"Cool, I'll see you then."

"How long did Chanel say she would be?"

"Thirty minutes. We can order some bottles, mingle with the birthday boy for a minute and leave in an hour or so. I ain't really tryna be out late tonight. Got mad shit to do in the morning."

"I'm following your lead."

"Then come on, Chuck, let's go." CoCo playfully grabbed Chuck's hand and went right past the line, waving at the front door security who all knew her by name and face. Lil Wayne was blasting through the state-of-the-art sound system as they maneuvered through the multi room club/lounge.

"Oh, lets chill in here," CoCo decided when they walked into the Tenshi Room. The lavish garden with natural Asian elements of bamboo, rocks, water and the reflecting swimming pool with a frog pond as the centerpiece of the exquisite garden had CoCo mesmerized. They found a sitting area right near the pool and she was more or less content. She only needed one more thing.

"Chuck, get that waitress's attention."

Chuck's six-foot six burly ass stood up, and with a slight wave of his hand had the waitress at their table in seconds.

"Hi. What can I get you?"

"Two bottles of Cristal Rose, and send a couple over to the birthday boy. Let him know it's from CoCo and Chanel."

"Will do. How will you be paying for this?"

"Cash."

"Great. How many glasses do you need for the table?"

"Bring six in case I want to share."

"Okay, I'll be back in a few minutes."

"The Compound got it going on?" Chuck asked CoCo.

"Yeah, they did some remodeling and the shit is hot. They have a couple of other rooms they're still working on, but it's fly. I was thinking that maybe Chanel and I should have our 25th birthday bash here. What do you think?"

"It could work. You'll have more than enough space."

"I was thinking maybe we could have a live performance in either the MB1 or Ride Patio room. It would be official it I got Lil Wayne or T.I. to perform. Shit, maybe both them motherfuckers. They'd shut the whole party down."

"If you wanna make that happen you need to start making preparations. Your birthday is only a couple of months away. You better get on it."

"I know you right. I'll talk to Chanel about it when she gets here. If she down for it, which I'm sure she will be, then I'll start placing those phone calls. Dang, here the waitress comes with our bottles already," CoCo said, noticing the waitress. "I can appreciate fast service."

"Here you go. Would you like for me to open both bottles now?"

"No, only one. My sister hasn't gotten here yet and Chuck here doesn't drink," CoCo smiled. After the waitress filled CoCo's glass and walked away, she quickly gulped down her champagne, ready to get her buzz going.

"Maybe you should slow down. Don't forget you have to save some for your sister."

"Chuck, that's why I ordered two bottles. This one is all for me." CoCo raised her glass up, and that's when the tall lanky figure dressed all in black caught her eye. What made CoCo observe his presence was because it was hot as hell outside but he had on a long sleeved trench coat. She shifted her eyes up to get a look at the fool who was rockin' a coat in the summer, but his hat was sitting so low she could only see the tip of his nose. CoCo glanced back down and that's when it hit her.

"CoCo, what's wrong?" It was clear to Chuck that something or someone had her full attention and he wanted to know why. Chuck turned his neck around to get the answer.

"Oh shit! I think that nigga coming for me!" CoCo exclaimed as the drink slipped out of her hands and the glass of champagne shattered on the table.

Chuck jumped up in front of CoCo to shield her and pulled out his gun, but it was too late. The perpetrator already released his bullets, and because his gun had a silencer, by the time the crowd knew what had went down he had made his exit.

"CoCo, stay down!" were the last words she heard before Chuck fell to the floor.

People in the crowd observed in confusion, wondering why this strongly built older man was laying on the floor until they saw the red blood oozing from his neck.

"Somebody call an ambulance! I need help over here!" CoCo screamed out. She was down on her knees shaking as she grabbed napkins from the table, pressing down on Chuck's wound to stop the flow of blood. But she knew it was all in vain.

Chapter Nine
California Love

Genesis woke up to a hard dick with a wet mouth around it. It had become an almost daily morning ritual that he looked forward to. Anytime Denise spent the night with him, which was becoming more frequent, this is what she bestowed upon him. Genesis knew it was her attempt to get him so spoiled from her services that he would decide to keep her in his back pocket, and her plan was beginning to work. With one hand caressing his balls and the other one massaging his dick as her mouth deep throated, Genesis was cumming in Denise's mouth within minutes.

"Baby, you make a nigga look extra forward to waking up in the morning."

"Thank you," Denise smiled after swallowing his cum.

"Listen, I have to go to LA tomorrow. Would you like to come with me?"

"Of course! I would love to come, thank you, baby." Denise jumped up in the bed and then gave Genesis a hug. "I've never been to LA before. I can't wait to go. How long are we going to be gone?"

"About three or four days."

"When I go in for work today, I'll let them know I need the rest of the week off."

"You don't think that'll be a problem, do you?"

"If it is, it's their problem. I ain't giving up a chance to go to LA wit' my boo for a little job at the retail store. Speaking of work, I need to go. I have to be there by eleven."

"Okay. Our flight leave early in the morning, so after work pack up whatever you taking and come back over here tonight."

"I will. Thanks again, baby." Denise blew Genesis a kiss before entering the bathroom to take a shower.

"Ring! Ring! Ring!"

Genesis grabbed his cell and saw it was Deuce. "What it is."

"You tell me. We still on for LA tomorrow?"

"No doubt. We got some serious business to handle."

"And don't forget some fun. I can't wait to hit up yo' man's, T-Roc party. I ain't tryna sound like no groupie, but I can't believe you cool wit' that dude."

"It ain't that serious. Our relationship is more business than anything. He's letting me invest some money in a new startup record label. It's an excellent look for both of us, but more so for me."

"I don't give a fuck. All I know is we 'bout to party wit' some Hollywood motherfuckers."

"Man, you trippin'. But Denise amped about going to

LA too, and I haven't even told her about the party. I'll let it be a surprise."

"Denise! You bringing Denise to LA wit' us?"

"Yeah, why what's the problem wit' that?"

"For one, I ain't bringing Tonya and she gon' be mad as hell that Denise coming and she not. You need to scratch the Denise thing."

"I already told her she was coming. I ain't gonna change that shit because you don't want to bring Tonya. I don't know why you don't bring her. She can keep Denise company while we handling business."

"Fuck that! I'm tryna find me a sexy bunny in LA. Maybe have a reason to visit more often."

"And I thought you was ready to settle down with Tonya and had gotten all that notorious whoring out your system."

"I am much more settled. Instead of having several side pieces, I only have a couple. Damn, you gotta give a brotha time. You can't expect me to completely cut off my new pussy radar."

"Nigga, you crazy. I'll talk to you later on."

As soon as Genesis hung up with Deuce, his cell went off again. "Hello."

"Genesis, it's me, CoCo."

"What up, CoCo? Is this a new number you calling me from?"

"No it's my home number."

Genesis was surprised CoCo was calling him from home, but knew it couldn't be about business. "Is everything straight with you?"

"No, it's not."

"What's wrong?"

"It's Chuck. He was killed a few nights ago."

"What! I'm sorry to hear that. By who? What happened?"

"I don't want to talk about it right now. I was calling because I'm not gonna be able to meet you in LA."

"Damn!"

"You go, though. Everything is still straight on that end."

"You sure?"

"Definitely. I spoke to my people and they know to be expecting you without me."

"I appreciate you looking out. But Chuck was a good dude. I can't believe I ain't gon' see that man again. How is Chanel? Can I do anything for both of you?"

"Chanel's okay. But I'm taking it the hardest since I was closer to Chuck than she was. We're going to have a small funeral for him and let that man rest in peace."

"Maybe I need to come. This LA trip can wait."

"No, go to LA. We both need that trip to happen. Try to stop through Atlanta on your way back."

"Bet. That's what I'll do. Text me the addy to where the funeral will be taking place. I want to show my respect and send some flowers."

"Will do. I'll see you soon."

"Cool. Give my best to Chanel."

After Genesis finished his conversation with CoCo he wondered who the fuck killed Chuck and if it had anything to do with the shooting that took place at that club months ago. Genesis decided that he would definitely stop in Atlanta after his trip to LA so he could find out what the fuck was going in the streets of ATL, and if it would interfere with the business he had going on.

Although Genesis and CoCo had become real cool in the last few months once he brushed off her bossy behavior, they were also knee-deep in their business relationship. CoCo and her sister were already banking major bread when Genesis came into the picture, but the mutually beneficial relationship had taken both to a new level of stackin' paper. Genesis didn't want anything to interfere with that.

Knowing that he was making a stop through Atlanta also got Genesis to having flashbacks about someone else—Talisa. It had been months since the last time he saw her, but in his mind it felt like yesterday. He had made a conscious decision to squash any chance of having a relationship with her but that hadn't erased her face from his mind.

"Baby, I'm about to leave. Good thing I brought a change of clothes with me or I would've never made it to work on time."

"Maybe you should start keeping some clothes here. I have plenty of closet space."

"Are you serious?"

"Why not? You stay here half of the week anyway. It doesn't make much sense for you to drive all the way on the other side of town to get clothes when you can keep some here."

"I couldn't agree with you more. See you tonight." Denise kissed Genesis goodbye and headed out the door with a smile on her face. Before she could even get to the elevator, she pulled out her cell phone to call her girl, Monica up so she could brag about her prosperous morning. When she stepped on the elevator and pushed the talk button, *searching for service* popped on the window.

Denise was anxious to share the news of her good fortune. When the elevator opened to the lobby, instead of trying to make her call again right then, she rushed to the parking garage. That was another thing she loved about staying over Genesis crib, because she was able to push his new black on black Benz and leave her old model Honda Accord at home. *The perks of fucking with a baller!*

The second Denise drove out of the garage she hit the talk button again. "Girl, guess where I'm going tomorrow!" Denise shouted into the phone.

"Besides work, I have no idea," Monica snapped, not appreciating the loudness from Denise's mouth that made her ear throb.

"California, baby!"

"What?"

"You heard me. This morning after I sucked my man off, he invited me to take a trip to LA with him. And he asked me to bring some clothes to keep at his crib. Watch, like I told you and Tonya a few weeks ago, that nigga gon' be asking me to move in."

Monica was speechless. She figured Denise was going to tell her Genesis was taking her shopping at this new expensive boutique they both were dying to got to but neither could afford, or some simple shit along those lines, but not this.

"Monica, are you there?" Denise thought maybe the call had dropped and was about to hang up and call back again to continue her bragging.

"I'm here. The phone accidentally fell on the bed," she lied.

"Oh, so you didn't hear my good news. Let me tell you again."

"No, I heard you. I dropped the phone after that."

"Isn't that shit the bomb, girl? I am too excited…"

"Umm, let me call you back, Denise," Monica said, cutting her off."

"Why?"

"That's my mom on the other line."

"Oh, okay, tell Ms. Parker I said hello."

"I will."

"I'll call you back during my lunch break."

"Talk to you then," Monica said before clicking over to the other line. "Girl, you will not believe what Denise just told me."

"What her simple ass talking about now?" Tonya asked, while lying in bed watching Jerry Springer.

"Genesis told her to start keeping some of her clothes at his place *and* invited her to go to LA with him tomorrow."

"Bitch, stop playing."

"I ain't playing. I was talking to her when you called, but told her my mom's was on the other line 'cause I had to tell you this bullshit. If that nigga move her in we won't be able to say shit to her ass. She already thinkin' she Helen of Troy."

"Girl, Deuce is going to LA tomorrow and he ain't even invite me. I begged that nigga to take me, and he told me it wasn't that kind of trip, it was strictly business. I knew he was lying 'cause his thrifty ass came home wit' some Prada and Gucci bags. This nigga going to LA to floss, probably scheming on some new pussy and leaving me here. I ain't gonna neva hear the end of this from Denise."

"That's for sure. Dude must be feeling homegirl."

"Or feeling all that sex she throwing on him. How the fuck did I end up with the loser of the two? Monica, let me call you back. I heard Deuce come in and he got some explaining to do."

Tonya picked up the remote control and hit the mute button, waiting for Deuce to make his way to the bedroom. She could hear him in the kitchen and was tempted to make her way to him, but decided to chill. A few minutes later he came strolling into the bedroom.

"I'm glad you up. You were sleep last night when I got home and I been horny all morning." Deuce took his shirt off and began unzipping his jeans knowing he was about to get some ass.

"You still going to LA tomorrow?" Tonya was hoping Deuce would say "no" and that would explain why he hadn't invited her to go.

"Yeah, so we betta give that mattress a good workout to hold you over while I'm gone."

"Deuce, I've never been to LA before. Let me go with you... please," Tonya said in her sexiest voice.

"Baby, I told you, Genesis and I are strictly doing business on this trip. I wouldn't have no time to spend wit' you."

"So why is Genesis bringing Denise if it's strictly about business?"

"I had no idea he was bringing Denise wit' him. I don't know what that's about."

"Stop lying, Deuce. You know good and well Genesis bringing her. Why in the fuck can't you bring me too?"

"Why you got to start some bullshit? I'm leaving

tomorrow so I'm tryna spend some quality time wit' you, and all you want to do is complain about some silly ass trip."

"You ain't tryna spend no quality time wit' me, you tryna fuck. If this trip is so damn silly, you wouldn't have a problem bringing me."

"I ain't bringing nobody."

"I've been fuckin' wit' you for a minute now and you don't neva take me no place but to bed. I'm tired of this shit. Genesis take Denise to nice ass restaurants, buy her Gucci bags, and flying her out of town, and I can't get nothin' but some dick from you."

"I ain't Genesis, and whatever he do wit' Denise is on him. That ain't got nothin' to do wit' us, so don't even start making comparisons."

"Whatever, Deuce," Tonya flipped her hand, getting out of the bed.

"Where you going? We was about to do our thang," Deuce said, halfway in the bed with his dick hanging out.

"You can do yo' thang solo, the same way you taking that trip to LA solo."

"So what, I can't get no ass 'cause I won't bring you to LA wit' me? Man, you trippin'!"

"No, you the trip. All you want is some steady pussy to run up in at your convenience. Well your personal convenience store is now closed. Enjoy your trip and forget my number."

"Fuck you then, Tonya! I don't need this bullshit no way."

Tonya ignored Deuce as he continued to ramble on, and got dressed. She was fed up with her arrangement with Deuce, especially when Denise was constantly rubbing in her face all the wonderful things Genesis was doing for her. Tonya's feelings did run deep for him, but it was evident that unless she made a move the shit in their relationship was never going to change.

****

"This place is more beautiful in person than it is on television," Denise said in complete awe during their Limo ride from the airport to the hotel.

"It definitely ain't Philadelphia, that's for sure," Deuce stated, opening one of the bottled waters in the ice bucket.

"So baby, what are we going to do today?" Denise was excited about exploring the streets of LA. She wanted to have a detailed list of events to boast to Monica and Tonya about.

"Deuce and I have some business to handle, then tonight we're going to a party."

"A party! I didn't bring anything to wear for a party."

"Don't worry, while I'm at my business meeting you can go shopping. Our hotel is right on Rodeo Drive."

"*The* Rodeo Drive? The one E News be saying all the stars shop on?"

"I guess, but I don't watch E News so I can't say for sure."

"It's gotta be," Denise said grinning.

Deuce sat back so damn happy that he didn't bring Tonya on the trip. Her hand would've stayed in his pocket because every time Genesis hit Denise off with some loot, she would have her hand out wanting the same thing. Deuce knew that Genesis was an extra generous type dude. He never had a problem with splurging, but unfortunately for Tonya that wasn't in Deuce nature.

When the Limo pulled up in front of the Luxe Hotel Rodeo Drive, Denise's eyes widened with anticipation. The driver opened the door for her and she tried to get out so fast she almost broke the heel on her sandal. She played if off and strutted to the entrance where she waited for Genesis, who was tipping the driver.

"This place is crazy sexy," Denise said when they entered the hotel.

A modern art collection graced the walls and the sleek décor struck you the moment you entered the lobby. The hotel had classic, chic boutique warmth with the elegance of Beverly Hills entwined. And it only got better when they reached the Penthouse Suite. Both the bedrooms and a separate parlor had double doors opening up to a private wrap-around sundeck that encompassed the entire floor.

"Look, baby. From here you can see where you'll be shopping," Genesis pointed out to Denise from the balcony, showing her the impressive views of Rodeo Drive and Hollywood Hills.

Damn, I can get used to living like this, Denise thought as she gazed out at her surroundings. "I'm going to find something sexy to wear tonight so you'll want to fuck me the whole time we're at the party."

"Don't get mad then when I tell you to meet me in the bathroom."

"I won't."

"A'ight, that's what's up then. But, I need to get going. I

left some money on the bed for you."

"When will you be back?"

"In a few hours."

"What time does the party start?"

"Around eight. Shit get poppin' early in LA and ends early too."

"Okay, baby, I'll see you later on. While you're out, I'll be getting pampered."

Denise sat on the bed counting the money Genesis left for her after he left. She reminisced about all the low level hustlers she had to fuck with to finally get where she is now. Dealing with bullshit to get a nigga to cover her half of the rent, or to pay to get her hair and nails done, to getting a couple of new outfits, all that to get nickel and dime the whole way. But not anymore, and it was all thanks to Tonya. If it wasn't for Tonya inviting Denise and Monica to his crib, she would've never met a nigga like Genesis. A man of his status wasn't hanging out at the clubs Denise and her friends frequented. On the rare occasion he would, he was holed up in the VIP section sitting in a corner discussing business. Denise was well aware of how lucky she was to be at the right place at the right time, and was determined to maintain her position.

****

"Excuse me, a rental car company was supposed to drop a car off for me. Did it get here yet?" Genesis asked the gentleman at the concierge desk.

"Are you Genesis Taylor?"

"That's me."

"Yes, it was delivered a few minutes ago. I was just about to call up to your room. You know we have a town car service here that would gladly take you anywhere you want to go."

"I know. I'll be using it tonight, but right now I need the rental car key."

"Yes, of course. The vehicle is parked right in front. It's the white Range Rover."

"Thanks."

As Genesis was on his way out of he noticed Deuce sitting on the chair in the lobby being extra animated with someone he was speaking to on the phone. Genesis tried to get his attention but Deuce was so caught up in his conversation it was useless.

"Man, I'll be out front," Genesis said, walking up on Deuce and catching him off guard.

Deuce put his finger up signaling to wait a second. "This silly broad hung up on me."

"Who?"

"Tonya nutty ass. I called her tryna be nice and she still trippin' because you brought Denise wit' you and I wouldn't let her come."

"Denise is cool and she don't bring me no stress. Your situation with Tonya, that's on you."

"True, but she takin' this bullshit to the next level. She saying that when I get back all her shit will be out my crib and she ain't fuckin' wit' me no more."

"You need to handle that."

"It's your fault. If you hadn't brought Denise none of

this shit would be happening."

"I ain't tryna hear that bullshit. Now get in," Genesis huffed, unlocking the Range. "I have more important things on mind like closing this deal."

"All you ever think about is making deals."

"What the fuck else matter? Without money your shit doomed anyway. And finally dealing with CoCo's connect myself is giving me the opportunity to make even more loot. I been waiting for this opening, but I do feel bad that Chuck had to lose his life for me to get it."

As Genesis headed north on Rodeo Drive, the comment Deuce made remained in the forefront of his thoughts. All he seemed to focus on was making deals to stack more money. That notion consumed his brain every day and night to the point he didn't have time or energy to enjoy anything else. Genesis stayed in a race against himself, never wanting to go back to what his life was.

The old Genesis was broke. Constantly worrying where his next dollar would come from and felt abandoned by the only woman he gave his heart to—his mother.

The new Genesis only cared about getting money, spending it the way he saw fit, and love wasn't even on his to-do list. That's what made Denise such an easy, perfect fit. Genesis knew he could never fall for a woman like her, but she fulfilled his sexual needs and he enjoyed her company.

****

Denise stalked out several exclusive and expensive retail

stores up and down Rodeo Drive. Most of the sales ladies gave her shade when she walked in until she gladly opened her purse to reveal she was holding more than enough dough to cop whatever she wanted in their store. Denise actually wasn't offended by the obvious snootiness since she was no longer in Philly, but in the upper echelon of high society. She was looking forward to earning her Hollywood socialite card and was going to have fun spending Genesis's money to get there.

After trying on several outfits that were stylish and pricey, none of them had that sexiness that Denise wanted to exude until she stepped into Roberto Cavalli.

"This is what I'm talkin' 'bout!" Denise cheered, filtering through endless racks of pure hotness. She grabbed about six different outfits to try on because the choices were nonstop.

As she browsed in *haute couture* heaven, she became mesmerized by a woman who came out of the dressing room wearing a light pink and orange/multicolor oversized, flower print, pure silk gown. It had a deep V-neckline, spaghetti straps, empire waist, and keyhole back and ruche bodice.

"That dress is gorgeous, and damn that's a bad bitch!" Denise further stated once she got past the gown and checked out the body and face of the woman in it.

"May I help you with your items?" the saleslady offered, snapping Denise out of her trance.

"Excuse me, I'm sorry. I was admiring the dress that woman is wearing."

"Yes, isn't it exquisite? And she looks fabulous wearing it."

"Who you telling. I would love to rock something like

that but that dress is too long for me. I would get lost in it. That lady has just enough height on her, so it fits her perfectly."

"So true. It's amazing on her, but I have a dress that would be killer on your petite figure. Follow me."

Denise happily trailed the saleslady, excited to see what she had in mind.

"What do you think?" The saleslady held up an above-the-knee-length sheath dress. It was cream with a tan/brown animal print. It had a square neckline with wide shoulder straps.

"This is the bomb!" Denise said, tossing the six outfits she was holding on the rack and grabbing the deliciously fly dress out of the lady's hand. "I'll have my man eating out the palm of my hand in this getup."

"I take you'll be getting this?"

"You got it!"

"Wonderful choice. Now it's shoe time. Follow me."

Again, Denise was delighted to follow the saleslady's lead. On their way to scope out shoes, she passed the woman she had been admiring and noticed a buff bodyguard with her. *Damn, who the fuck is that broad? I ain't never seen her on TV or nothing, but she must be somebody serious with security and shit tailing behind her ass*, Denise figured.

****

An hour after getting her dress, shoes and accessories, Denise made her departure from Roberto Cavalli. She looked down at her watch and had enough time to stop by the nail salon for a manicure and pedicure. She had gotten her hair freshly trimmed and colored before leaving Philly so she could handle the maintenance. She strolled down Rodeo Drive with bags in hand feeling like the official wifey of a Kingpin, and loved it.

Chapter Ten
Since You've Been Gone

"Whose party is this? Damn, they got a red carpet and all these paparazzi and shit," Denise said, stepping out of the car stunned by all the hoopla. She was thrilled that she picked out the dress she wore because she felt that not only did she blend in with the rest of the Hollywood elite, but stood out as a red carpet showstopper.

"A business associate," Genesis informed her, casually making his way to the front door as if this was just another party for him.

"Yes, are you on the guest list?" an uptight doorwoman questioned, holding a clipboard.

"Of course."

"Name please," she countered, as if not convinced.

"Genesis Taylor."

After scrolling down the list her eyes widened. "Mr.

Taylor, hi. One moment, I'll get the hostess to escort you to the VIP area." Suddenly her frosty attitude flipped to kiss-ass status.

Deuce and Denise were like lost puppies with their tongues hanging, mimicking every step Genesis took as they were shown to their table on the upper level where the VIP area was. They sat down on the plush seats, and each table already had bottles of champagne decorating them. From the balcony you could see the lower level where people were getting their dance on to the sounds of DJ Cassidy.

"This is some official shit right here!" Deuce said across the table to Genesis. "There's so many young bunnies up in here I don't know where to start."

"Nigga, you crazy. Always on the prowl," Genesis laughed, then saw T-Roc walking up on him.

"My man, Genesis. I'm glad you came through." T-Roc gave him a slight hug. "Are you being taken care of? Do you need anything?"

"I'm good. This party is nice, but I wouldn't expect nothing less from you."

"Yeah, It's a pre-celebration for an upcoming movie I'm about to start filming."

"Movie! Let me find out you doing films now. That's major. What type role is it?"

"Leading man, starring opposite of Tyler Blake," T-Roc proudly revealed.

"Tyler Blake who starred in 'Angel' with Andre Jackson? I loved that movie!" Denise interjected, not able to contain her excitement.

T-Roc smiled. "Yes, that Tyler Blake."

"This is Denise and that's Deuce," Genesis said, realizing

he hadn't introduced them yet to T-Roc.

"Nice to meet you both."

"T-Roc, if you don't mind me asking," Deuce said with a grin.

"Please, what is it?"

"Is Tyler Blake as gorgeous in person as she is on the big screen and in magazines?"

"Even more."

"Get the fuck outta here!" Deuce waved his hand and they all laughed.

"Is she coming tonight?" Denise wanted to know, hoping it could be one more thing she could brag about when she got back to Philly.

"She was invited, but knowing Tyler, I doubt it. She's a homebody. Not really into the Hollywood scene."

Fuck! I'll have to cross that one off the list, but at least I can tell everybody that I got to meet T-Roc's fine ass. Tonya and Monica are gonna be so heated, Denise reasoned.

"I'm not going to hold you up. I know you have mad people to do that Hollywood schmoozing with, but we'll definitely talk later on."

"No doubt. It was a pleasure meeting all of you and enjoy the party," T-Roc said before walking off.

"That's a cool nigga right there. He got all the fame and paper, but down to earth. I see why y'all get along," Deuce said, nodding his head in approval.

"Wow, Genesis! I can't believe you know T-Roc. You really must be doing the damn thing, baby," Denise added her two cents.

"I so wanted to ask that nigga if he was twisting Tyler Blake scrumptious ass out, but felt it would be inappropriate."

"You damn right, nigga!" Genesis was ready to clown Deuce.

"One of the tabloids I read said her man is Andre Jackson so I doubt T-Roc is hittin' that," Denise said.

"You and your tabloids. You can't believe all that bullshit you read." Genesis brushed off Denise's comment. As he was about to pour everybody some champagne, Deuce nudged his hand.

"Yo, look who's coming over here." Deuce lifted his chin up and Genesis turned to that direction. He swallowed hard as the past came walking into his present.

"Genesis... CoCo's friend, correct?" Arnez said, reaching out his hand to Genesis.

"That's right. We a long way from Atlanta and here we are meeting up again. I take it T-Roc is a friend of yours?"

"Actually not. I was in town on business and an associate of mine told me to come through. Glad I did. I see you're in the big leagues now, making moves."

"Nah, just maintaining," Genesis replied in a humble tone but giving a clear indication that "you know it, nigga". "Oh, my fault. This is Denise, and you remember my partner, Deuce."

Arnez nodded his head, "One moment. Here comes my fiancée now." Arnez turned around grabbing her hand. "You remember Talisa?"

Genesis almost choked seeing Talisa again. When he didn't see her with Arnez from the jump he wanted to believe that they were no longer together, but now he saw that wasn't the case. To make it worse, Arnez addressed her as his fiancée.

"Oh yeah, I do remember her. How's everything?"

Genesis asked, casually extending his hand politely, wanting no one to know how sick he felt at that moment. But Deuce could always read Genesis and saw that he still had the same infatuated glaze from the first time he saw her at the airport in Atlanta.

"Everything's great, and you?" Talisa reached out to reciprocate the gesture and both could feel the undeniable chemistry flow through their hands as they connected. Talisa quickly pulled away knowing Arnez's jealous streak and wanting to avoid a lashing when they got back to the hotel.

"I see someone I need to speak to, but it was nice to see you again, Genesis. We have to set up a time when we can sit down and discuss doing business together," Arnez suggested.

"No doubt. I'll get your number from CoCo."

"Do that. Enjoy your evening."

"Who was that?" Denise had to be nosy.

"A gentleman in the game."

"He must be doing it big in the game."

"Why you say that?" Genesis was curious to see where that statement came from.

"Because when I was at the Roberto Cavalli store earlier today picking out this dress I'm wearing, homegirl was there trying on that exact gown she has on and she had a bodyguard with her. Only a nigga clocking serious bread is going to have his wifey escorted by a bodyguard."

Genesis watched as the couple went downstairs to the lower level. Emotions of jealousy, anger and resentment flooded him and he hated it. Talisa was not his woman and never had been, but he felt that she was supposed to be with him and not Arnez.

He turned around and watched from his seat as the two of them walked across the floor and over to two gentlemen. Arnez sat down and appeared to be in a deep discussion with them. Talisa whispered something in Arnez's ear and headed towards the ladies' room.

"Can you both excuse me for a moment?"

"Where you going, baby?" Denise was becoming more territorial of Genesis and loved the idea of being the main bitch. She didn't want any of the bevy of beauties in the party to make a move on her man.

"I have to speak with T-Roc for a moment and he's downstairs. I'll be back. Deuce, keep Denise company while I handle something."

"No problem." Deuce wasn't stupid, and if he was a gambling man he would bet every dollar in his pocket that Genesis was going to chase after Talisa.

Genesis took the back way around the club, not wanting to cross paths with Arnez and avoiding being in Denise's line of sight. When he got to the ladies' restroom a Spanish woman was parked in front as if guarding the door.

"Did you see a beautiful black woman, about this tall," he said putting his hand to his chest, "Wearing a long gown go inside there?"

"Yes," the woman nodded.

"This is yours if you make sure no one else comes in until we come out," Genesis said, peeling off a couple of hundred dollar bills.

"No problem!" she said, snatching the money in case he changed his mind.

When Genesis entered the bathroom, Talisa was standing

in front of the mirror expressionless. She was so deep in thought she didn't hear him come in.

"What is weighing so heavy on your mind?"

Talisa jumped, startled to realize she wasn't alone. "Genesis! What are you doing in here?"

"I had to talk to you."

"You can't be in here. What if someone comes in?"

"I took care of that," he said, coming closer to Talisa.

"Genesis, you can't be here. Plus I'm sure the woman you're with wouldn't appreciate you being in the bathroom with me," she said, unable to mask her jealousy of seeing Genesis with another woman.

"Don't worry about that. I'm right where I want to be. Why didn't you ever call me?"

"I wanted to but…" Her voice trailed off.

"But what?"

"It doesn't matter."

"Why, because you're engaged now?" Genesis grabbed Talisa's arm and held up the hand that had the ten carat sparkler on it.

She stared down, not responding.

"Look at me!" Genesis demanded.

"Why… what do you want from me Genesis?" she asked, still not making eye contact.

"I want you. Seeing you here, I can't let you go this time." Genesis reached in to kiss her but Talisa turned away. "I know you feel something for me too. I'm not crazy."

"Don't you understand? It doesn't matter. I have to go."

Talisa broke away from his grasp but Genesis pulled her back in. "Do you still have my number?"

"Like I said, it doesn't matter."

"Answer the question," he insisted in a forceful tone.

"Yes," Talisa answered quictly as if not wanting to admit it.

"I'll still be in LA tomorrow. If I hear from you then, I know these feelings ain't one sided. But if not, I'm done. That's my word." Genesis let Talisa's arm go and she rushed off, not looking back.

Genesis stood in the bathroom unsure of what Talisa's next move would be. He could read women enough to know there was a mutual attraction, but whether she would act on it had him stuck. He wrestled with why Talisa was holding back and his gut told him it had nothing to do with being in love with Arnez. Although Arnez had a hold on her, he remained puzzled as to why.

****

"Let's go!" Genesis barked when he got back to the table where Deuce and Denise were sitting.

"You ready to go now? But, baby, we haven't even been here that long," Denise protested with a confused look on her face.

"You're welcome to stay, but I'm ready to go. Deuce, what you doing?"

"Man, I'ma chill for awhile. I'll hit you up later on or early tomorrow."

"Cool. What you gon' do, Denise?" Genesis asked, as if he didn't give a fuck one way or the other.

"I'm leaving with you. We came together so we

leaving together."

Genesis headed downstairs, not saying a word to Denise. It was apparent he had a salty attitude; about what, Denise couldn't figure out. On their ride over to the club, the nigga was feeling up her leg, telling her how hard she had his dick in the bad ass dress she was sporting, and now he was treating her like she had the monster. The flip in his actions had her scratching her scalp.

"Genesis, why all of a sudden you acting shady? What happened in there that got you so vexed?" Denise asked on their way back to the hotel.

"It's nothing," he said, shrugging her off.

"No, it's something. One minute you can't keep your hands off of me, and now I'm pulling tryna get two words out of you. When you went to speak with T-Roc, did the conversation go faulty or something?"

"Look, this ain't got nothing to do with business. I don't feel like talking, and if that's what you want to do, then I suggest after the driver drops me off you have him take you back to the party 'cause I ain't got no conversation for you."

Denise was stunned by the blatant disregard Genesis was showing her. She had never seen that side of him. But she realized that they had never been in a situation of conflict before. It was always either sex, going out to dinner, shopping or a she-coming-he-going type deal. She had never questioned Genesis before and he had never been put in a position to answer her. Now that Denise was trying to put any sort of demand on him, no matter how small, she was getting a close-up view of his reaction.

Not wanting to fuck up the comfortable style of living she was growing accustomed to, Denise decided to fall back and not press the subject any longer. Genesis had some shit on his mind and clearly he didn't want to discuss it with her. She sat back in the car and followed his lead, which was complete silence. She knew all about a nigga and his mood swings, so she would have to ride this one out until he snapped out of it.

****

The next morning Denise woke up and watched Genesis, who was still sleeping. She was tempted to give him the standard crack of dawn treatment which consisted of her signature blowjob, but was skeptical after how distant he was last night. Even after they got back to the hotel and she took a hot shower, oiling her body up and coming out naked with glistening skin, that nigga rolled over, shut his eyes and didn't breathe in her direction. That shit shut Denise's self esteem down. She didn't know if she could take back-to-back rejection like that.

"Fuck it! Let me order something to eat." Denise was tired of staring at Genesis so hard as if it was going to make him move. She got out the bed to get a menu to quench her stomach hunger.

"Get back in back," she heard Genesis say, surprising the hell out of her.

"Huh?"

"You heard me, get back in bed."

Denise had no intention of refusing his request, seeing every muscle ripple against the off-white sheets. She crawled back in bed and headed downtown to give him what she figured he missed the most.

"Nah, I need to be up inside you." Genesis wanted to let off some frustration, and having Denise do all the work wouldn't allow that. He pulled her up and tossed her down on the bed and began pounding on her insides, releasing the anxiety he had over seeing Talisa and losing her again all in one night.

"Oh shit, baby!" Denise moaned, loving the beating he was putting on her pussy. She figured he had gotten over whatever had him in a funk, and she played her cards right by not stressing him.

Genesis continued his thrashing as his anger began subsiding with each vigorous stroke. Denise clawed her nails in his back down to his rock hard ass, pushing him further inside her until it felt as if his dick was about to come up through her throat.

"Damn, I love my dick!" Denise purred, thinking that her bomb ass pussy was the reason for the pouncing she was getting, not knowing she was only a mere substitution for what he really yearned for. She could feel Genesis's body throbbing and prayed that he would bust off inside of her.

"Baby, cum inside of me!" she whispered in his ear, dying for Genesis to bless a seed inside of her.

Although he was zoning in the wet juices, he was lucid enough to pull his dick out and spread his seeds in her mouth and not her reproductive system.

Being the consummate stack chaser that Denise was, she swallowed all his cum up with an expression of pleasure stamped on her face as she raged with disappointment inside.

Genesis lay on his back looking up at the ceiling, feeling complacent. He wanted to reach for a cigarette but had been trying to kick the habit and didn't want to backslide.

"Baby, that was the best fuck ever," Denise smiled, stroking her finger down his chiseled sweaty chest.

"Yeah, it was exactly what I needed."

"Me too. So what are we going to get into today... I mean besides each other?"

"Ring! Ring! Ring!"

"Bookmark that," Genesis said, reaching for his cell phone. He didn't recognize the New York City area code but picked it up anyway. "Yo."

"Hi, it's me, Talisa. Are you busy?"

"No. Where are you?" Genesis got out of bed with the quickness and excused himself to the private terrace, bypassing Denise like he had not just twisted her brains out a mere few minutes ago.

"I'm in the lobby of our hotel."

"Where's Arnez?"

"He had to go out for a meeting. He should be gone for a couple of hours."

"Can I see you?"

"Yes. Can you come now?"

"Yeah. What hotel are you at?"

"Beverly Wiltshire."

"That's a step away. Give me twenty minutes. Do you want me to meet you in the lobby?"

"No. You can meet me at this restaurant off Rodeo. I'll call you when I get there and let you know where it is."

"Alright, I'll see you shortly." Genesis hung up with Talisa with renewed energy. He walked back in the room and Denise was in bed waiting patiently.

"So, baby, what are we doing today?" she asked again.

"I have to go."

"Go where? I'll come with you."

"No, it's business."

"I thought you handled all your business yesterday."

"So did I but something came up and I have to go manage it."

"When will you be back?"

"I don't know. I'll leave you some money. Go shopping or something." Genesis went in the bathroom and slammed the door.

"What is up wit' that dude? One minute shade, then he fucking the shit out of me, and now it's back with the cold shoulder. Either that nigga suffer from that DID personality disorder I heard about recently, or something or somebody have him going in circles," Denise said out loud, determined to get to the root of the bullshit.

****

Talisa walked down Rodeo Drive continuously looking over her shoulder, afraid that at any moment Arnez would sneak up on her and shut down her chance of spending time with Genesis. In her mind she knew he was nowhere in the vicinity, but paranoia had been embedded in her by the actions of a man she loathed and feared. That's why after staring at Genesis's number on numerous occasions in the past few months, she never had the nerve to follow through with a phone call. But her chance encounter with Genesis changed all that. Talisa couldn't fight her urge to see him knowing he was so close within her reach.

"Where are you?" Talisa called Genesis the second she reached her destination after being seated in the back of the quaint restaurant and ordering a drink.

"I'm on Rodeo. Where are you?"

"The Armani Café on Brighton Way."

"I'll be there in a matter of minutes."

"Are you walking?"

"No, driving."

"Okay, when you get here come straight to the back. I'm sitting at a table in the corner."

"Alright, bye."

Talisa sipped on the Bellini she ordered nervously. There was this combination of school girl crush jitters mixed with second thoughts of reaching out to Genesis in the first place. But that reluctance ceased when she saw him coming towards her. There was no denying how much she wanted him.

"That was quick." Talisa stood up and kissed Genesis on the cheek.

"I told you I was only a step away," Genesis said as he immersed in the sweetness of her perfume. "You look beautiful as always."

"Thank you."

"Are you blushing?" Genesis teased.

"Shut up! You're not supposed to call me out like that." Talisa put her head down feeling embarrassed.

"I'm sorry, you're right. I couldn't help myself. I guess

it's hard for me to believe a woman who looks like you could blush about anything."

"Oh please, Genesis. I get embarrassed about too many things."

"Like what? Tell me."

"Not now, we don't have that much time."

"You have to leave?"

"Yes, I have to be back at the hotel before Arnez gets there."

"Fuck Arnez! You don't need him. Things are so much different for me now than when we first met. I can take care of you. I know you used to an over-the-top lifestyle, and now I have the money to give it to you on the same level as Arnez."

"I'm not with Arnez for his money and I wouldn't be with you for yours."

"Then why do you stay wit' that cat? I can tell you ain't happy wit' him. So if you're not staying for the money, then what?"

Talisa let out a deep sigh but remained silent with her words. She wanted to tell Genesis the truth and confide in somebody about the torture and abuse Arnez had been unleashing on her, but she was afraid Genesis would look at her as some pathetic, weak woman.

"It's complicated," she said instead.

"Then let me make it uncomplicated." Genesis glided his hand across the table and put it on top of Talisa's. "You called me for a reason. I know you're ready to give us a try. Don't fight it, just give in."

"You make it sound so easy."

"It is. We give it a shot and see what happens. I'm

confident that I'll make you extremely happy and I believe you'll do the same for me."

"What about the girl you were with last night? You all appeared cozy."

"That's nothing. She can't stop what I want to have with you, if you let me."

Talisa gazed at Genesis's face and she believed he was sincere. His words and eyes were telling the same story. "Okay, I want to try," she admitted, throwing caution to the wind.

Genesis broke out a wide smile but kept his suave swagger in check. "That's what's up! I'll put my lady friend on a flight back to Philly today and we can stay here for a few days and spend some quality time together."

"I would like that, but what do I tell Arnez?"

"Don't tell him anything. Go to the hotel and get your stuff before he gets back. Then call me and I'll come pick you up. Or if you want, I'll take you to the hotel now and wait for you."

"No, I can go by myself."

"You sure?"

"Yeah. It'll also give you some time to straighten out your own situation." They both smiled.

"Cool. How long do you think it'll take you?"

"Give me an hour at the most."

"And that's all I'm giving you. I promise, after today I'ma change your life forever."

"That's a huge promise, but for some reason I don't doubt it coming from you."

"I knew you were a smart girl. Now go get your shit so we can start working on that new life."

Genesis leaned over and Talisa met him halfway as their lips rested on one another before their tongues interlocked. The passionate kiss both longed for had finally happened and it exceeded both of their expectations.

****

When Genesis got back to the hotel he spotted Deuce sitting on the couch cheesing up to some semi-cute girl in the lobby. In a rush to get Denise on a plane to Philly, he decided to skip speaking to his boy and went straight to the elevator.

"Yo, Genesis, hold up!" Deuce yelled out, noticing Genesis right before he was about to step onto the elevator.

"Damn!" Genesis shook his head not having time for small talk.

"Man, you didn't see me sitting over there?"

"Yeah, but I have to hurry up and take care of something."

"Business, I'm sure."

"Actually, I need to get Denise to the airport."

"You leaving today? I thought we weren't breaking out for a couple of days."

"No, Denise is leaving today. I'm staying."

"You slick motherfucker!" Deuce smiled. "You hooked up wit' Talisa, didn't you?"

Genesis couldn't contain his enthusiasm. "Yeah, I just got done meeting up with her and we're going to spend some time here in LA together, see where we can take this."

"I'm proud of you man. That persistence paid off, not to

mention any broad that can get you take a break from work is a'ight wit' me."

"Speaking of broads, who is shorty over there?"

"This chick I met last night at the club after you left. But she ain't showing a nigga no California love."

"What's the problem?"

"She stayed the night in my hotel room last night, didn't let me hit the skins—fine. I take her to the fly ass restaurant in the hotel for breakfast this morning thinking we can follow it up with some sexing. But this treasure hunter telling me she want to go shopping on Rodeo Drive and want me to foot the bill. I was over there tryna convince her that first we go have sex, then I'll take her shopping. This trick ain't stupid, she already know that after I hit it the only shopping she would be doing is for a cab home."

Genesis burst out laughing listening to the clownism coming from his friend. "I guess that means you'll be pulling out that cash."

"Hell no! I ain't tricking on the chick. She cute but not that cute. I'ma try one more time and if she ain't complying it's time for her to go. I might be on that flight wit' Denise so I can go home and beg Tonya to take me back. At least I know I can get some ass without breaking my pockets."

"As pissed as Tonya is with you, that might be your only option."

"Shit, I rather trick on Tonya who has shown some loyalty then this new pussy over there tryna hustle me out my coins."

"I feel you. Let me know what you doing 'cause I'm trying to have Denise out of here in the next thirty minutes."

"There's no way I'll be ready by then. If I leave today

I'll take a later flight. But I'ma hit you up regardless to let you know what I'ma do."

"Cool." Genesis got on the elevator checking his watch to see how much time he was working with. Denise had played her role long enough and the gig was up—it was time for her to go.

When he got to the room, Denise was still laid up in the bed in the same position he left her in. The television was on and she was munching on the food she ordered from room service.

"Hey baby, I'm glad you back. I was missing you. I called you a couple of times but you didn't answer your phone."

"Yeah, I was focused on my meeting."

"Well, now that your meeting is over you can focus on me." Denise got out of the bed, strutting her naked body over to Genesis. She wrapped her arms around his neck and reached in to kiss him.

"Listen, something came up and you need to pack your stuff up so you can make this flight," Genesis said, pulling Denise's arms from around his neck.

"So I can make a flight? You're not coming with me?"

"No, I have to stay here."

"Then why can't I stay here with you?" This time Denise was not trying to hide her disgust with what was coming out his mouth. She popped her hip out and folded her arms wanting an explanation.

"Because I don't need any distractions."

"I won't be a distraction. I'll stay out your way."

"I know, and to guarantee that, you going home."

"Genesis, what is really going on?" Denise voice was

rising and her anger was visible.

"Nothing is going on. I told you I need to take care of some shit and you need to go the fuck home."

"Is it another bitch? Is that what this bullshit is about? You been going from hot to cold since last night and this lip service you giving me ain't cool."

"This ain't about no other woman," Genesis lied, wanting to avoid a showdown. He didn't need the hassle with the time he was working with. "Now I need for you to pack up your stuff so you can make this flight. I already made the reservation. If you miss the flight because you standing here tryna stress me over some bullshit, I'ma be pissed."

Denise could tell by the tone of Genesis's voice that he was giving her a not so subtle warning. She didn't want to roll the dice and take a chance that he wouldn't fuck with her anymore because he was turned off by her aggressive attitude. She hoped that he was telling the truth and it was business that had him shipping her out instead of some new pussy he was anxious to swim up in.

"Fine. Let me get my shit together. The last thing I want to do is piss you off because I miss my flight."

She gathered her belongings and took a quick shower with Genesis hovering over her, reminding her every second to hurry up. She didn't realize until they got downstairs and the car service pulled up that he wasn't taking her to the airport or even going along for the ride. Denise felt jilted, and not even the stack of cash he stuffed in her purse made the blow any less painful.

"I'll call you," were his departing words before slamming the door shut.

"Bye," Denise snapped back at him.

Genesis waited a few minutes making sure the car was in route to its destination before heading back inside the hotel.

He then went to the front desk. "Hi, my name Genesis Taylor and I'm staying in the Penthouse suite. I need for my room to be cleaned immediately."

"No problem, sir. I'll have that taken care of right now."

"Thanks." He glanced at his watch and then looked at his phone to make sure he hadn't missed Talisa's call. He figured she would've made contact by now.

Three hours later, and still no call from Talisa. Genesis sat on his bed perplexed and livid. He had even got so fed up that he called her, but her cell went straight to voice mail. He was tempted to leave a message, but no matter how pissed he was, he didn't want to start any shit between her and Arnez.

He paced his room scrambling to figure out what went wrong. He then got in the car and drove past the Beverly Wilshire and waited, but he didn't see Talisa or Arnez.

Did she have second thoughts and decide to stay wit' that nigga, Arnez? Why the fuck would she play these type of games with me? Maybe something went wrong and she couldn't call me...but what?

Fed up with wondering and waiting, Genesis went back to his hotel with more questions and no answers.

Chapter Eleven
Give The Game Up

The loud ringing of his cell phone woke Genesis up. He had fallen asleep with it right next to him in anticipation that Talisa would call, but that never happened.

"Hello," he groaned half asleep.

"You an early bird. I can't believe you still sleep," CoCo huffed in the phone.

Genesis eyed the clock on the nightstand. "It's only nine o'clock here, but I do need to get up."

"Oh, my fault. I thought you would've left Cali by now since you already had that meeting."

"Yeah, I was gonna chill here for a little while, you know, relax."

"You get in some relaxation, that's a first. It's always about business for you. But Arnez did tell me he saw you chillin' at this party in LA, so maybe you are loosening up some."

Hearing CoCo mention Arnez's name made Genesis fully wake up quickly. "I did run into Arnez the other night. He suggested we hook up and discuss some business. I told him I would get his number from you. When did you speak to him?" Genesis kept his voice in an even tone and casual so CoCo wouldn't know he was searching for answers.

"He actually stopped by last night. He said him and Talisa had come from the airport a few hours earlier."

"Oh." *So she went back to Atlanta wit' that dude. What the fuck is going on wit' this chick?*

"So what's up? Are you coming to Atlanta before going back to Philly? I really wanted us to sit down and talk. There's a lot of shit going on."

"I'm coming. I'm about to call the airline and get the first available flight."

"Damn, you must really miss me. I knew for sure you were going to postpone the visit."

"CoCo, I got you. You need me, I'll be there."

****

Genesis arrived in Atlanta with one purpose on his mind—finding Talisa. He did want to get the inside scoop on what was going on with CoCo, but Talisa was at the top of his agenda.

As he made his way through the airport towards the car rental spot his phone started ringing. He looked down wishing it was Talisa, but it was Denise. She had been blowing up his phone since last night and he was now officially annoyed the fuck off.

****

"I can't believe this nigga ain't picking up my calls!" Denise screamed at the phone then slammed it shut. Right when she was about to toss it across the room in frustration it started going off.

Maybe this Genesis calling me back, igniting herself with hope until recognizing the number. "Hey Monica."

"Damn, that's the type of greeting you give your best friend?"

"I'm a little annoyed that's all. What's going on?"

"I'm headed over to the Pier to have lunch and drinks. Come meet me over there."

"Girl, I ain't in the mood. I'll see you when you get home."

"Come on, getting out will do you some good. Ain't no fun being stuck up in the house annoyed. Some good food and a drink make everything better."

Denise glanced at herself in the mirror and she was already dressed. Hanging out with Monica would help her to stop stressing over Genesis for at least a couple of hours. "A'ight, I'm on my way."

When Denise hung up with Monica she tried calling Genesis one more time hoping to strike up some luck, but once again came up short.

****

Genesis parked his rental in the parking garage of the condominium complex CoCo and Chanel lived at on Peachtree Street.

Her spot was the ultimate in high-rise living and reminded Genesis of floating in the sky every time he would visit her place. He was so enamored with the breathtaking rooftop, two bedroom, two and a half bathroom penthouse that it was the inspiration for purchasing his crib in Philly.

"Genesis, you made it!" CoCo said, opening the door and beaming, happy to see her business associate and someone she considered a friend, which was rare in her occupation.

"What's going on, lovely?" he said, giving her a hug and kiss on the cheek.

"When I spoke to you earlier, I meant to thank for the beautiful flowers you sent. That touched me," she said, closing the door behind them.

"It was the least I could do. I can't believe Chuck is gone. He was a good dude and he always looked out for you and Chanel."

"He was. Do you know he died saving my life?"

"What? You didn't tell me that."

"That's why I wanted to speak to you in person and tell you what the hell was going on. Follow me into the kitchen. I was about to make me something to eat."

Genesis trailed behind CoCo on the custom made walnut floor, and his eyes instantly shifted to the bird's eye maple cabinets because it accented the complete Viking kitchen perfectly. It also included a motorized flat screen wireless

TV that emerged with a push of a button.

"So yeah, we were at the Compound for a birthday party and out of nowhere this dude pulled out his piece and tried to take me out. If Chuck hadn't jumped in front of me I would be the one six feet under right now." CoCo got choked up thinking about it.

"Did you see who it was?"

"No, his hat was pulled down too low over his face. He had the shit set up tight because that nigga came in and disappeared out like a ghost."

"Where was Chanel? She ill wit' her shit. She didn't have nothin' for that nigga?"

"If she had been there, I'm sure she would've. We got to the party first and were waiting on her to come when the shit went down. Chuck died in my arms, Genesis. I ain't gonna ever forget that shit."

"I know, it'll be okay." Genesis held CoCo closely as she disclosed a vulnerable side to herself to him for the first time.

"That's the thing. I don't know if it's going to be okay."

"Why not?"

CoCo freed herself from Genesis and opened the refrigerator door, fidgeting with the food nervously. "I didn't want to tell you before because we were just getting to know each other."

"Tell me what? And stop messing wit' that food. You making me uneasy."

"Sorry."

"Don't be sorry. Tell me what's going on."

"That night at the party, whoever did that shit was aiming for me. This makes the second time in the last few months that someone has tried to kill me. And it ain't no coincidence."

"What, you know who it is?"

"I'm not sure. But you know that connect you met with in LA? A lot of niggas want to get at dude because his product is prime and he get it for dirt cheap so you can't beat his prices. But Quentin don't fuck wit' too many cats, that's why I never introduced you to him. But, umm, under the circumstances, I didn't have a choice. Plus, I trust you enough that you wouldn't try to cut me out once you build your own link with him."

"How were you able to connect wit' dude?"

"My father."

"I didn't know your father was in the business."

"He was. He died a few years ago. He rolled with some major players and Quentin Jacobs was one of them. On the strength of my father he has looked out for me and my sister—product wise—lovely."

Genesis nodded his head taking all the fresh info in. "What does your relationship with Quentin have to do with somebody tryna kill you?"

"About six months ago I got a call from someone wanting to discuss business with me. I set up a meeting and me, Chanel, Chuck and another one of my guards were all there. Two young niggas showed up saying that they were representing for their boss who wanted to stay anonymous."

"He wanted to do some business wit' you and use them as the go between?"

"No, the Mr. Anonymous not only wanted a direct linkage to my connect, but he also wanted me to not fuck wit' him no more."

"I'm lost. You mean stop getting your drugs from Quentin but let *him* get them?"

"Exactly. I thought the shit was a joke and we all laughed our asses off. But the two men were very serious. They said the price that I was able to give niggas on the streets was fucking up their boss's operation. So after I finished laughing I told them cats to get the fuck out and tell their boss to kiss my ass."

"And you have no idea who their boss is?"

"No, and never did I think he would come at me like this—hard... blazing."

"Well, you need to find them niggas who came to see you and torture they ass until they give up their boss."

"I've been on it and so has Chanel, but like the dude who killed Chuck, them niggas are ghost too."

"Can't no nigga get ghost unless they're dead. Not finding them just mean that you looking in the wrong place."

"True, but Genesis, I'm scared. I'm tryna be strong because I don't want Chanel to wig out and start killing every suspect nigga that cross my path. But this is the part of the game I prayed I would be able to avoid."

"We'll figure it out."

"We have to because I don't want to die."

****

When Denise arrived at the restaurant on the Pier, Monica was already sitting down munching on appetizers and sipping on a margarita.

"Hey girl! I was beginning to think you had changed your mind and wasn't coming," Monica said, standing up and giving Denise a hug.

"Nah, you were right, I needed to get out of that damn apartment. Chilling outside on the pier and having some drinks was the perfect idea. Excuse me, can I get a Long Island ice tea?" Denise said, waving down the waitress.

"A Long Island this early in the day! You really must be annoyed."

"And it's about to get worse." Denise rolled her eyes pissed that her nerves was about to get further worked.

"Hey ladies, I see the party has already started without me." Tonya sat down at the table.

"Why didn't you tell me she was coming?" Denise glared at Monica not even giving Tonya any rhythm.

"I wasn't sure if you were going to show up and I didn't want to drink alone."

Denise smacked her lips over the whole entire set.

"Denise, no need to be rude, it ain't my fault that there is trouble in paradise. I'm sure it ain't even that time of the month, but you over there feeling pain worse than menstrual cramps due to your boo. Have a few more drinks. I'm sure it will numb the sting."

Monica leaned back in her chair sizing up both of their body language before digging in. "Okay, what the fuck is going on?"

"Nothing," Denise cut in trying to dead the conversation before it had a chance to start brewing.

"Oh, Denise didn't tell you why her trip to LA got cut short."

Monica twisted her neck so hard it damn near snapped

when she turned towards Denise to get the lowdown.

"There ain't nothing to tell. Genesis was flooded with business and was too occupied so I decided to come back home. End of story."

"That's the story you running with, Denise? Monica, are you riding with her version or do you want the raw and uncensored one?"

"Tonya, why don't you shut your miserable ass up? You mad 'cause Genesis took me on a fly trip to LA and Deuce left your ass here."

"Well, my man brought his ass back home to me last night after realizing the grass definitely ain't greener on the West Coast. What's Genesis's excuse for shipping yo' ass back here and he staying in LA?"

"I already told you, although I don't owe you no fuckin' reason."

"No offense, Denise, but I want one," Monica chimed in.

"I already gave it to you. Tonya bitter ass want to hear herself make idle chatter. She ain't got shit to tell you."

"I supposed that means you already know the reason Genesis was so quick to put you on a plane was so he could spend time with his real boo, which clearly ain't you."

Monica spit out her drink, caught off guard by the bulletin report Tonya shared.

"You a lie!" Denise yelled.

"By your reaction, that would make Genesis the lie. I guess all that sucking and fucking you was bragging about a few weeks ago is no longer doing the trick," Tonya mocked.

As if on cue the waitress came up with Denise's drink, but instead of it ending up going down her mouth it was used to give Tonya an unsuspecting shower.

"Take that, you lying bitch!"

The waitress ducked away quickly, not wanting to get caught in the middle of whatever drama that was sure to go down.

Monica was speechless as Tonya's black eyeliner and mascara smeared down her face and her Farrah Fawcett flipped hairdo went to a wet doggy shag.

"Bitch, I'ma kick yo' ass like a bad habit!" Tonya lunged across the table, knocking over the ketchup bottle, plate of appetizers and other condiments.

Luckily for Monica, she was quick enough to move her Margarita out of the line of fire before the chaos broke loose.

Tonya gripped Denise's neck so tightly that when she fell back in her chair hitting the wood flooring, Tonya fell right along with her.

Denise jerked her body erratically and so determined to get out of Tonya's clutches that it sent the ladies tumbling violently down the stairs. Denise's petite frame was about to fly away like a piece of paper in the strong wind when they reached the bottom. But Tonya made sure that wasn't going to happen when she reached over and seized the top crop of her hair, putting Denise in a headlock.

"Yo' little bitty ass always poppin' so much shit like can't nobody fuck you up!" Tonya said tightening her grip.

"Tonya, let her go! They about to call the police on the both of you." But Tonya was so furious over the drink episode she wouldn't budge.

Denise was flinging her arms trying to keep hope alive, but Tonya's stocky ass was strong and her lock was firm.

Monica had no choice but to start grabbing on Tonya's

arm, trying to make her let go of Denise's neck. "Tonya, stop playin' and let go of Denise's neck!"

"Ain't nobody playin' wit this cunt!" Tonya released her hold on Denise and let her fall to the cement.

"Are you okay?" Monica asked, helping Denise up. She nodded her head "yes" although her outer form was edging towards broken down. Both of them had minor cuts and bruises after taking equally dramatic tumbles.

The people on the pier who had gathered around to get an up-close view of the girls gone wild brawl were now dispersing, getting back to their own business.

While Monica dusted her friend off, Tonya used the opportunity to get her shit and break out in case the police had been called. Monica paid the bill and tried to calm Denise down. Denise wasn't sure what had her more heated; the scuffle with Tonya or finding out that Genesis was open off the next bitch.

****

Genesis sat outside drinking a Corona and taking in the stunning 360-degree panoramic view from the sweeping wrap-around terrace. There were four unique soaring turrets that provided dramatic views of downtown Atlanta to the south, Stone Mountain to the east, and Buckhead just to the north. The relaxing vision soothed his senses and made him hunger for Talisa. He figured with the alone time he had while CoCo was taking a shower he should try to reach out to Talisa again.

The phone rang several times with no answer, but Genesis was relieved the shit was no longer going straight to voice mail. When he was about to hang up there was a breakthrough.

"Hi," Talisa said, softly.

"You finally turned your phone back on. What the fuck is up wit' you, Talisa?"

"Genesis, I'm sorry."

"I don't want to hear no motherfuckin' sorry. You had me waiting for your call all night. And I find out you un brought yo' ass back to Atlanta. What type of shit is this? I thought we were done playin' games."

"We are."

"I can't tell."

"I do want to be with you Genesis. I was going to call you in a few days and try to come to Philly and see you."

"You can come see me right now."

"I can't come to Philly tonight."

"I'm not in Philly, I'm in Atlanta. Now are you going to see me or not?" There was a long pause filled with silence. "Answer me, Talisa."

"Not tonight, Genesis. In a couple of days I'll come to Philly...I promise."

"I'm fed up wit' your promises. Either I see you tonight or I'm done for good this time."

"Fine. Tell me where to meet you."

"I'm at the Four Seasons."

"Okay, I'm on my way. I'll be there in a half hour."

"Don't bullshit me, Talisa."

"I'm not. I'll be there. Bye."

Genesis hung up not knowing what to make of this

shit. But he knew all this back and forth had to come to an end tonight. He wasn't into juvenile games and wasn't going to play them with Talisa even if that meant walking away for good.

"Are you hanging out with me tonight or what?" CoCo walked out on the terrace with a silk nightie and matching mid-thigh robe.

"Maybe another time. I can't tonight."

"I understand. When are you going back to Philly?"

"Probably tomorrow but it all depends."

"You will call me before you leave, right?"

"No doubt, and CoCo, don't worry. Everything will be okay. We will get to the bottom of this bullshit and figure out who is after you and is responsible for killing Chuck."

"Thank you."

"No problem. I'll call you tomorrow."

CoCo walked Genesis to the door and it hit her that she would be sad when he left. And it wasn't the "I miss my friend" sad, it was "damn, I wish I could fall asleep in my bed with that fine motherfucker beside me holding on tight". She couldn't help but wonder if maybe there was a chance that she and Genesis could take it beyond a friendship and become intimate. As far as she knew he wasn't seriously involved with anyone, and she assumed he was over his infatuation with Talisa since he hadn't mentioned her in months. At that moment she decided it couldn't hurt to try and ignite a potentially seductive flame.

"Hey, sis!" Chanel said coming through the front door and snapping CoCo out of her daydreaming.

"Chanel, you scared the shit out of me! I didn't even hear the door open."

"You can lighten up, it's only me." Chanel walked into the living room and slid off her stilettos, relaxing on the couch. "I ran into Genesis when I was getting off the elevator."

"Yeah, I needed to discuss a few things with him."

"Business things?"

"Some business. What happened with Chuck, and that someone is trying to kill me."

"Why would you tell Genesis that?"

"Because it's true and he needs to know."

"Why?"

"Chanel, we do business together and we're friends."

"Friends! When did you start becoming friends with business associates? That was on your top five not-to-do rules."

"It's different with Genesis."

Chanel went over to the bar and poured some Hennessey in two glasses. She walked over to CoCo and handed her a glass and then sat back down, crossing her sculpted mocha-chocolate colored legs.

"CoCo, I know you ain't put your guard down and got hot for that nigga, Genesis," Chanel said in her true ice-cold composure.

"Girl, stop trippin'."

"Don't run that shit wit' me. I'm your sister, your twin sister. That shit all in your face, the way you say his name, you feeling that dude."

"And what if I am?"

"Cut the shit out now. We do business wit' dude, that's it, nothing else."

"It doesn't have to be that way. My relationship with

Genesis is different than with the other people we deal with in this business. We care about each other."

"Do you hear what the fuck you saying? We deal with killers, drug dealers, niggas that would take out their own mother if the price was right." Chanel leaned her body out to directly face CoCo, stressing her point.

"I know what type of people we deal with, but Genesis ain't like them."

"Maybe it's time for you to get out the game," Chanel suggested, matter-of-factly.

"Where the fuck did that come from?" CoCo stood up on the defensive.

"I know you've been stressed, and Chuck's death hit you hard. Now you talking about starting a relationship wit' a nigga we work with. Maybe you ain't cut out for this business no more and you need to venture off into something else."

"Then who would run our shit?"

"I can maintain it. You know I love having my hands all up in the gritty shit."

"But you don't even like to talk to people when we negotiating business. All you wanna do is be the enforcer."

"Listen, if I have to step up to the plate to keep shit in order, then that's what I'll do. And if that means communicating wit' niggas, then that's what I'll do. I can play any position, but right now we talking about you. You seem to be getting soft and that's not good."

"You acting like I'm in a full-fledged relationship wit' Genesis. Ain't nothing even went down between us."

"But the fact you would even consider it lets me know you slippin'. You know I'm right. A few years ago this would've never crossed your mind no matter how fine the nigga was."

CoCo stood in front of the soaring glass window staring out at the gorgeous sunset at dusk. She wasn't sure how to take the logic her sister was spitting at her. Was she slipping and did she need to step away from the street life once and for all? If so, would Genesis be willing to do the same with her? She doubted it. He seemed to love the allure of the game and making money way too much. But then again, you never know.

Chapter Twelve

We In This Together

Genesis was checking his voice mail when he heard knocking at the front door of his hotel room. After deleting the tenth hostile message Denise had left him, he tossed his phone on the bed, regretting he ever fucked with her in the first place.

"I have to admit, I'm surprised you showed up," Were the words Genesis greeted Talisa with when he opened the door.

"You didn't leave me much of a choice."

"If you didn't care one way or the other, then I did."

"But I do care and you know that. Now are you going to make me stand in the hallway or can I come in?"

Genesis moved to the side. Talisa brushed pass him and sat down in the living room of the L-shaped suite.

"Can I get you something to drink?" he asked her.

"No, I'm fine."

"Well, you can relax."

"I'm relaxed."

"Then put your purse down and take off your shades. You're not outside anymore."

So that's what Talisa did, and Genesis regretted he asked her to do so when he saw her face.

"What in the fuck happened to your eye?" Genesis bent down beside the chair Talisa was sitting in and held up her face. "Is this why you didn't want to see me today?"

"Yes," Talisa admitted, nodding her head.

"Who did this to you? Was it Arnez?" Talisa stayed mute. "Answer the fuckin' question. Did Arnez fuck up your eye like this?"

"Yes, he did."

"When did it happen?"

"Yesterday when I went back to the hotel, he walked in on me when I was packing to leave. We got into an argument. I told him I was fed up and couldn't do this anymore. So of course like always, he knocked the shit out of me." Talisa nervously folded her hands as she confided for the first time what had been transpiring in her personal life. She thought she would feel as if a weight had been lifted, but instead she felt naked, as if all her vulnerabilities were being exposed.

"*Like always*...how long has this nigga been putting his hands on you?" Genesis's jaw was tightening and his anger was overtaking him.

"Too long. I'm so tired of this bullshit. I don't even know who I am anymore."

"Damn, Talisa! You shoulda told me what was going on. This nigga over there hittin' on you and shit. I wanna kill that motherfucker!"

"I couldn't tell you or anybody else. I feel stupid. Never did I think I would be the poster child for abused women."

"Don't blame yourself. A real man don't beat up on no woman. That nigga a punk." Genesis had flashbacks of the beatings he witnessed his mother succumbing to for all those years. Getting an up-close view of the terror his father reigned over him and his mother using violence, Genesis hated any man who raised his fists to a woman.

"Yeah, but it doesn't change the fact that I put up with this shit for so long."

"It's never too late. The ball's in your court. What's your next move?"

"I want to leave Arnez for good and never go back."

"Then make it happen."

"Genesis, you make it sound so simple."

"I'm telling you it is. Where dude at now?"

"I'm not sure. He got a phone call that seemed urgent and he hurried out and took security with him, which left me home alone."

"And that's when you left."

"Yeah, he had me under his thumb since we got back from LA. When I got the opportunity to break out I did."

"Where were you going?"

"Honestly, I wasn't sure, but I knew I had to get the fuck outta that house. I couldn't take that shit anymore. I was gonna go stay with my parents but I didn't want to bring the drama to them. Then when you called I was going to come see you in Philly once my eye was healed."

"I'm leaving for Philly tomorrow. Come with me."

"Are you sure?"

"I've never been more sure of anything in my life."

"Genesis, when Arnez realizes I'm gone he's gonna come looking for me."

"Let him. And I hope he brings his punk ass to Philly. I got sumthin' for that nigga."

"Arnez, is crazy. I don't want anything to happen to you because of this foul predicament I've gotten myself into."

"Crazy is as crazy does and I can bring it just like that nigga can. Don't worry about me. Only question you need to answer is if we in this together or are you going to be on some indecisive shit and go back to Arnez.

"We in this together."

"You sure?" Genesis cupped Talisa's face in his hands. Her eyes were filled with tears.

"I'm sure," she said without hesitation.

"Why are you about to cry?"

"Because for the first time in so long I feel hope, and you've given me that."

Genesis knelt down and gently kissed Talisa's lips. Then he pulled back to feel her out and see if she wanted him to stop or continue. When she leaned forward with desire in her eyes, Genesis knew it was fair game. Their lips and tongues connected, igniting the burning desire each had been harboring from the moment they met. Genesis slid his hands up Talisa's thighs, stopping at her silk panties. His finger glided inside, becoming covered in her juices.

Talisa's hips gyrated as Genesis stroked her pussy intensely. "Baby, I want to feel you!" she said breathlessly, with the finger fucking no longer being enough.

"I want you too," Genesis whispered as his tongue circled her earlobe. He then scooped her up from the chair and carried her into the bedroom, laying her down. He stared at the outline of her body as it draped the bed.

"Don't keep me waiting, please!" Talisa started unbuttoning her shirtdress eager to have Genesis inside of her.

"Stop!" Genesis grabbed Talisa's hand. "Let me do it," he said as he took over where she left off, slowly unbuttoning her dress. When he got to the last button he opened the dress exposing her taut breasts sitting perfectly in the crimson silk bra. He unclipped her bra and filled his mouth with hardened nipple.

"Baby, I want you inside of me!" Talisa begged.

Instead, Genesis pulled her head back, kissing down her neck, chest, and stomach before sliding off her panties, massaging the lips between her legs with his tongue. "Ahhh!" she moaned, spreading her legs wider and pushing his head deeper as his tongue hit spots that had her entire body shivering. Right when Talisa felt her craving was being fulfilled, Genesis stood up and took off his shirt and pants, revealing every defined muscle Talisa had imagined he was working with underneath his clothes. Her eyes danced down to his third leg and her mouth instantly wanted to taste his rock-hard tool, but he had other plans.

Genesis slowly manipulated his long, thick dick inside Talisa's sugar walls, and for the first time let himself bond with a woman. His mind became lost with each stroke, savoring how wonderful it felt, making love for the first time.

****

"Girl, this nigga ain't answering my calls. How dare he ignore me!" Denise screamed out to Monica who was laughing her ass off on the inside but gave the sympathetic face on the outside.

"Calm down, Denise. Maybe he taking care of business and can't answer his phone."

"Fuck that! That motherfucker couldn't have been taking care of business since I left LA. He dodging me. I didn't want to believe Tonya, but I bet you that nigga laid up wit' that bitch right now."

"Now you letting your imagination get the best of you. Tonya didn't even say who this chick is and you over there visualizing Genesis being laid up wit' her. Come on now, chill out."

"So why he ain't returning my calls? He got about twenty missed calls from me and almost as many messages."

"Shit, you probably scaring the nigga off."

"Fuck it! I'm going over to his crib. His trifling ass might be back from LA and at his place wit' the bitch." Denise grabbed her purse and car keys.

"Okay, you 'bout to cross the line into stalker territory. If you go over to his crib what you gon' do?"

"Fuck that bitch up!"

"Denise!" Monica called out her name and paused, letting her know it was time to regroup. "You need to put your shit down and have a seat. This shit was funny at first but now I'm concerned."

"Funny? What's funny about my man ditching me in LA

so he could be with some other bitch? And then have to listen to Tonya rub the shit in my face. Ain't nothin' funny about any of that shit."

"I understand you vexed, but we need to go over a checklist before you take this scorned woman shit too far."

"What you mean a checklist?"

"A list of shit to see if you can validate this crazy behavior jumping off right now."

"Yeah, I can validate it. That nigga practically asked me to move in wit' him before he took me on a trip, and spent a grip so I could be fly at a motherfuckin' T-Roc party. He treated me like I was his woman."

"The key words are, 'like his woman' but you're not. And he didn't ask you to move in with him, he said you should keep some clothes at his crib. Again, that ain't the same thing. And as far as him spending paper so you can look fly at T-Roc's party or any other time is irrelevant. Genesis's paper is long. That ain't nothing for him. Plus, I doubt he want to take you to a high-class shindig looking busted, so of course he gonna make sure your gear is tight. That don't mean he wifed you, it means he wants the company he keeps to look official in his presence."

Denise tossed her keys and purse on the coffee table and then slouched down in the sofa. "So we clear, Monica, are you saying I'm just another trick to Genesis and nothing more?"

"Don't put words in my mouth. I didn't say that."

"Basically, that's what it sounded like to me."

"Damn, Denise, you acting like you a newbie in this game. It's like that night Genesis chose you over me. I wasn't happy about it—on the real I was pissed. That nigga fine and rich. Shit, I wanted him for myself. But he didn't want me, he wanted you, so I had to dust my shoulders off, maintain my composure and get the fuck out his crib. It wasn't easy but that's part of the game."

"What part of the game are we playing now?"

"We ain't playing shit. That nigga got all the money so he got all the power. I know you thought that your pussy and head game gave you the power, and it did give you a little, that's how you were able to go on that trip and get some expensive trinkets out the deal. But that's where it ends. Anytime you out here wheeling and dealing your pussy wit' these hustlers it's a gamble. You get what you can get, and when the ride is over your ass keep moving wit' some dignity. That means no running up on his crib tryna fight the next chick he's decided to play the game with."

Denise put her hands on top of her head shaking it back and forth. "I can't believe this bullshit. Genesis was supposed to be the one. I was this close to sealing the deal."

"Girl, besides fucking him, what other deal were you trying to seal? Wait, hold up!" Monica crossed her arms and tapped her foot on the carpet. "You thought you was gonna be the one?"

Denise looked up at her best friend. "Why is that so surprising? Why couldn't I be the one?"

"Child, please. That little innocent girl role you play might work on a wet behind the ear nigga, but Genesis got some miles on him. No matter how angelic the face and sweet the pussy, that cat can spot a get-money chick when he see one. He wanted to have fun with you and he did. You both enjoyed each other's company. You turning what was supposed to be a cool fling between two people into some fatal attraction type shit."

"So you telling me to let it go."

"Yeah, for now. I mean he might come back around but he won't if he think you can't control your emotions. The last thing a dude like Genesis want to be involved in is some stressful pussy. I got that from how he reacted to me at his crib that night. My in-your-face attitude was a turn off to him, but that's who I am. Your laid back approach was probably more his speed, but now you trippin' like y'all four kids deep wit' each other."

"I might be wrong, but I feel that Genesis is supposed to be mine."

"Well girl, I felt the same way when I used to go to the 76ers games and watch Allen Iverson play. But every time I looked up in the stands and saw his wife wit' all those damn kids, not including the ones he had on the side with his jumpoffs, I knew I had to get over it, and so do you."

Denise heard what Monica was saying to her but it didn't register. See, Denise had entitlement issues. She thought she was entitled to any man she wanted, and that included Genesis. The idea of him preferring another woman over her was simply not plausible. Denise had learned a tremendous amount of fucking skills while out on those streets whore hopping and used every single one on Genesis. His dick was supposed to be on lock with her being the only freak with a key, but unfortunately the sex skills she'd obtained only ran so deep for a man like Genesis.

****

When Tonya woke up the next morning she could hear Deuce on the phone running off at the mouth. She pretended to still be asleep so he would continue his yapping. He never liked her to get an earful of his conversations, and most of the time Tonya didn't care to anyway, but this topic was right up her alley.

"When you get back in town, we need to handle some things. What time is your flight getting in?" Deuce asked in between smoking on his "appetite enhancer".

"We're supposed to arrive around three o'clock."

"*We!* Who coming back wit' you?"

"Talisa."

"Talisa?" Deuce responded in shock. "You a slick nigga. How you get that chick to leave her man and come chill in Philly wit you?" Deuce chuckled and coughed at the same time.

"Don't worry about all that."

"So what, y'all a couple now?"

"Let's say we coming back to Philly to work on it."

"I have to give it to you, Genesis, you don't waste no motherfuckin' time."

"Shit, I ain't got time to waste. But I gotta go. Talisa is getting out the shower and we got a few things to take care of before we leave Atlanta."

"If I knew you were stopping in ATL, I would've come too, just to lust after them fine ass twins."

Tonya wanted to smack Deuce across his head for that statement, but decided to clobber his ass another time, knowing with his dumb antics the opportunity would present itself soon.

"A'ight, you better watch it. You know Chanel will come for that ass with a quickness."

"I know. That's what be turning me on about her sexy motherfuckin' ass. She got that whole militant vibe going. She the type of chick you be wanting to smack that ass good when you laying that pipe down from the back."

Tonya couldn't take one more second of Deuce's whoring ass mouth and decided to shut his ass up. "Damn, I got some good sleep last night," Tonya yawned, rising up in bed and stretching her arms out purposely knocking the spliff out of Deuce's hand.

"Fuck, Tonya!" Deuce hollered out in pain when the spliff fell out of his hand and burned his upper thigh.

That's what you get for lusting after the next bitch when you lying up in the bed beside me wit' yo' silly ass! she smacked.

"I'll see you when you get back," Deuce yelled in the phone before hanging up on Genesis. "Tonya, ain't you gonna help me?"

"You seem to have everything under control," Tonya said, casually getting out of the bed and walking to the bathroom.

When Tonya got in the bathroom her face lit up when she looked in the mirror. She couldn't wait to blab the new news she obtained from eavesdropping on Deuce's conversation. Not only did Tonya now have a name for Genesis's new boo, but he was also bringing the chick back to Philly with him. With that,

Tonya jumped in the shower, ready to head over to Denise and Monica's crib to further lunge the knife deeper into Denise's over-inflated ego.

Chapter Thirteen
Side Effects

"Baby, are you going to be okay here by yourself?" Genesis asked Talisa as he was preparing to make his exit. Genesis felt bad about leaving her at his condo so soon after getting back from the airport, but he had important business to handle with Deuce and Antwon.

"I'll be fine. I'll keep myself busy going through your drawers looking for incriminating evidence," Talisa smiled.

"I don't know what you think you're gonna find."

"I know you've had plenty of women keeping you company."

"Not me. I'ma saint, you didn't know." Genesis gave Talisa a devilish grin and did a quick check in his head to make sure that no one, mainly Denise, had left any sort of female give-away signs around his crib. He knew that

Talisa was well aware that he had women in his life prior to her. But after they made love last night, this was a fresh start for both of them and he didn't want anything to mess that up.

"Yeah, I know all about saints," Talisa teased. "But go head, handle your business. I'll try not to snoop too much."

"Do whatever you like. This is your home now too. I want you to be comfortable."

"Genesis, we don't have to live together. I can stay here temporarily until I get my own place. I'm not sure if I even want to live in Philly and I don't want to impose on your space."

"Listen, we agreed to give us a try. And there isn't a better way to see if it can happen then with us living under the same roof. Also, I can keep my eye on you here and I know you'll be safe from Arnez."

"Okay, you've convinced me, which wasn't hard to do. Let's do this. Trust, I can easily get used to falling asleep in your arms every night."

"Now we're on the same page! Now come over here and give me a kiss before I leave." Genesis held out his hand and Talisa gladly obliged giving him a goodbye kiss.

"I'll see you later, baby."

"Cool. If you need me for anything call me."

"I will."

When Genesis left out, Talisa went outside on the balcony and stared out at the mesmerizing panoramic view. The afternoon breeze swept over her skin giving a calming affect.

She did feel as if this was a new beginning and

one she would share with Genesis. No longer would she have to live in fear, wondering what would trigger Arnez to beat the crap out of her. Those days were gone. The more she thought about it, maybe living in Philadelphia wouldn't be all that bad. She could register for school in the local area and get her degree, which she knew would make her parents happy. Yes, Talisa was finally seeing life in a positive light again, something that seemed out of reach recently.

The sound of her cell phone ringing snapped Talisa's out of her deep thoughts. She went back inside and retrieved her phone off the living room sofa. She looked at the screen and it read "Private".

My parents probably got my message and are returning my call, she thought.

"Hello."

"I was beginning to think that you must be dead because there is no way you would ignore my calls. But I was wrong. You're very much alive... for now." Arnez's voice was as cold as his threat. "And don't even think about hanging up," he added as if reading Talisa's mind.

"Arnez, it's over," she announced in her most convincing voice.

He returned her statement with a ridiculing laugh, then quickly flipped to a tenor of evil, "Bitch, it's over when I say it's over."

"Your threats don't work with me anymore. You can take your sadistic behavior and fuck yourself with it. I'm done. The shit is past tense."

"You think you can hide from me, huh? This relationship is like the mafia—the only way out is death."

"Well motherfucker, consider me dead to you."

"Not until I personally break your neck."

Then the line went silent. Talisa sat down on the couch and her legs were shaking. She talked a big game to Arnez, but on the inside she was scared shitless. She knew how demonic he was and would do everything to hunt her down like a dog. But knowing Genesis was on her side is what gave her strength.

****

What was supposed to have been a ten minute shower, getting dressed and a quick ride over to Monica and Denise's crib for Tonya, turned into an all morning and part of the afternoon babying session for Deuce. He whined about the minor burn he encountered when she purposely knocked the spliff out his hand. Then he got his typical munchies, but instead of wanting some fast food like he normally did, he insisted that Tonya go in the kitchen and whip him up a hot home cooked meal. He wanted steak, eggs and some grits. When Tonya finished slaving over the hot stove and he finished his meal, this fool turns around and wants sexual services. Tonya's only saving grace was that Genesis had called and wanted to meet up with Deuce to discuss business.

I been trying to get my ass over here all damn day. Thank fuckin' goodness I finally made it. But nothing was gonna stop me from personally delivering this news to Denise's trifling tail, Tonya thought as she stepped out of her car.

She took her time walking to their apartment, smiling at the defeated stare that she would soon see decorating Denise's face.

"I'll get it!" Monica called out from the kitchen when she heard a knock at the door. She looked out the peephole and saw it was Tonya.

"Hey girl!" Tonya said, scooting her way pass Monica.

"Girl, what are you doing here? Denise is home and you know she don't want to see you."

"Shit, this ain't just Denise's place, you live here too. I can't come see you?"

Monica let out a sigh and slammed the door, knowing that Tonya was up to no damn good. "Tonya, what do you want, and it betta not be a fight. With my tax refund and stimulus check I got a new living room set and this carpet cleaned. Ya' ain't fuckin' my shit up wit' no blood and sweat."

"Girl, please. Been there and done that with Denise. I'm moving on to better things."

"Like what?" Monica questioned, but before Tonya could respond Denise came out her bedroom looking heated to see her face.

"What the fuck are you doing in my apartment? You need to go," Denise said pointing to the door.

"Denise, this is you and Monica's apartment."

"Bitch, that ain't nothing but a minor technicality. You need to get the fuck out."

"I'm glad to see that busting your ass down those stairs at the pier hasn't stopped all that bravado you got going on."

"Okay, that's it. Now I'm asking you to leave,

Tonya, because if any of my new shit get fucked up, I'm beating both of you bitches' asses. So let's just avoid that nonsense now, and you get the fuck out, Tonya, and I'll talk to you later."

"Fine, I'll leave, but I only wanted to come over and forewarn Denise so her feelings wouldn't get hurt."

"Forewarn me about what?" Denise popped.

Monica glared at Tonya wanting to tell her to keep the shit to herself, but her nosiness was getting the best of her, so she didn't intervene.

"Genesis is back in town."

"And?" Denise said, snapping her neck.

"He brought his new boo with him. Her name is Talisa."

Denise's mouth dropped. "Don't play wit' me, Tonya."

"Again, it's not me doing the playing, it's Genesis. I heard him on the phone with Deuce this morning. He was in Atlanta with her and their flight got in this afternoon. From what I understand they trying to work on being a couple."

"This motherfucker cannot be seriously playing me like I'm Bobo the Clown!" Denise was talking to herself out loud, steadily pacing back and forth across the room.

"It ain't no secret that we don't like each other, but I would hate for you to go to his crib and look like a dummy 'cause he un moved the next chick in. That ain't cool." Tonya continued adding layers, making Denise even sicker.

Denise's face turned beet red. "I can't believe this nigga! One minute he telling me to leave some of my clothes over at his place, and the next he shacking up wit' some bitch named Talisa. He ain't gonna get away with this bullshit!" Denise stormed into her bedroom.

"Was that really necessary?"

"Monica, you know you loved every minute of it."

"I enjoy juicy gossip like the next chick, but Denise don't need to get caught up in no more drama."

"That's what I'm trying to avoid."

Monica rolled her eyes at Tonya's blatant lie.

Denise came storming out her bedroom with mission stamped across her face. "Monica, have you seen my car keys?"

"Are these them?" Tonya jingled the keys in the air that she lifted from the glass television stand.

"Stop being so damn helpful," Monica snarled. "Where are you going, Denise?"

"To find out what the fuck is going on," she said, snatching her keys out of Tonya's hand.

"You already know what's going on. What else do you need to find out?" Monica was blocking the front door hoping to talk some sense into Denise.

"Monica, would you move please?"

"Not until you tell me what you about to do."

"I need to see Genesis so we can talk."

"You can do that right over the phone."

"But as you know, his punk ass ain't accepting my calls."

"Then maybe that's a clue you need to let it go."

"I'll let it go when I see him face-to-face and he tells me it's over."

"Denise, this is a bad idea. If you go over to Genesis's crib, you fuckin' up any chance you might have of dealing wit' dude again."

"That's a chance I'm willing to take. Now would you please move!"

Monica reluctantly stepped to the side clearing the way

for Denise to leave. Denise slammed the door so hard on her way out it looked like it knocked off its hinges.

"Are you satisfied now?" Monica directed her question to Tonya.

"It ain't my fault she let herself get caught up in Genesis. Remember, she was the one smashing that shit all up in our faces about how she had that nigga sprung. From where I'm standing she appears to be the one that's sprung."

****

Tears were burning Denise's eyes as she pressed down on the gas, speeding to get to Genesis's crib. Anger and embarrassment had blurred her judgment. She needed visual and audio confirmation that Genesis had indeed moved on. Not only that, Denise wanted to see the woman that had knocked her out the box with such ease.

Her sweaty palms gripped the steering wheel as she swerved in and out of lanes, almost hitting passing cars determined to get to her destination swiftly. The sounds of disgruntled drivers blowing their horns didn't deter her reckless driving. Denise only had one agenda and that was to confront Genesis and his new boo.

****

Genesis pulled up to the warehouse he purchased in

northeast Philadelphia. It was his covert hideout where he operated and discussed important business. When he arrived, he noticed both Deuce and Antwon's cars were parked on the side. He was relieved there would be no waiting because he wanted to wrap up their meeting as quickly as possible.

"We on time and you late. That's a first," Deuce said when Genesis came through the metal door.

"It must be love," Antwon joked. "Deuce filled me in on how you moved honey up here with you."

"That's what you clowns were discussing while in here waiting for me…my love life? You niggas need to be telling me about some new spots you setting up to put more paper on the table. Shit, I know everybody else in a recession, but that shit don't never apply to prostitution and drug operations. Motherfuckers gonna always want their dick sucked and their head lit up."

"Nigga, you crazy, but you know we stay making moves. Deuce just wanted to let me know that our boss had got lucky in love, that's all. Man, we happy for you."

"Yeah, maybe now you'll ease up on always stressing over work. I try to tell you life too short."

"Deuce, you be exaggerating. We kick it, have some drinks and shoot pool every week."

"Once a week. Don't make it seem like it's an every day occurrence. It don't need to be.

"While we be slippin' the next nigga is chippin' the fuck up. We play this shit right we can all retire from this game sooner than later. I know I'm ready to chill out and be done with all the stress that comes with this illegal shit. But for now there is too much money to be made out in these streets for all that. Speaking of money, that new connect we met with in LA will have our order ready in the next few weeks. So when we get the word, Antwon be ready to hit the road with the van. I want you to pick up the shit and be out."

"Am I going to the regular spot in Atlanta?"

"No, it's a new joint in Memphis. Before the connect was shipping from California where it was imported from Mexico then to Atlanta, but now it's changing up. He's going to have the drugs packed in boxes and coolers and shipped to a fake address in Memphis. He has a guy who works at Fed-Ex and he intercepts all shipments sent to the fake address and will hand-deliver them to you at an undisclosed address."

"Tennessee, here I come! Maybe I'll hit up Beale Street, find me a southern bunny and listen to some blues."

"No, this trip is strictly business. You can chase some ass on your own clock."

"Chill, Genesis! I got you. I'm in and out."

"Cool. When it get closer to the day I'll give you the address where you'll be meeting the Fed-Ex guy and a phone number in case you have any problems finding the location, which you shouldn't."

"This shipment Antwon is picking up, are we giving any to CoCo and Chanel?" Deuce asked.

"From what I know right now, nope, but that might change. If so, Antwon, after you leave Memphis you would make a stop through Atlanta."

"That ain't nothing. That's what, a four or five hour ride tops?"

"But I should know if you need to do that in the next few days.

I got a whole slew of niggas fiending for some product, so I'll get to dispersing the moment Antwon get back," Deuce said.

"Deuce, I like the sound of that."

"Yeah, well I'm about to be on a grind for a minute like you," Deuce nodded his head towards Genesis, "Stackin' my coins up."

"What's the motivation behind that?"

"I think I might ask Tonya to marry me."

"Nigga, don't make me fall out my chair. Is some love shit floating in the air out here in Philly or somethin'?" Antwon asked.

"Antwon, man, I'm serious."

Genesis was trying to read Deuce to see if he was spitting real talk. "What brought this on?" he asked to see if this was another one of his friend's comical routines.

"After that fiasco with that fake broad in Holly*weird*, I developed a greater appreciation for my relationship with Tonya. Plus, I got enough kids and baby mamas running around out here. If I don't slow my roll, I'll be able to start my own football team. It's time for me to settle down. Shit, I ain't getting no younger."

"I feel you, partner," Genesis patted Deuce's back.

"I feel you too, but marriage...that's one commitment I'm staying the fuck away from. Something about a female having papers on me brings the word 'prisoner' to mind. But Deuce, I wish you the best of luck," Antwon said to him.

"Thanks, man, Bow are we done here? 'Cause I'm hungrier than a motherfucker."

All three men laughed as they headed out going their

separate ways.

****

The pounding on the front door startled Talisa as she stepped out of the shower. She wrapped a towel around her and went to see who was making all the noise.

"Who is it?" Talisa shouted out before reaching the door.

"Will you please open the door? It's imperative I speak with Genesis." The calm sweet voice was in complete contrast to the loud knocking.

Talisa looked out of the peephole but couldn't see the woman's face, only the top of her head. "I'm sorry, Genesis isn't here," she said after opening the door.

"You!" Denise said softly.

"What about me?"

"You were the woman I saw at the Roberto Cavalli store and at T-Roc's party."

Talisa tried to place the woman's face and then remembered she had seen her at the party with Genesis. "Genesis isn't here so you should probably give him a call."

Denise pushed open the door, knocking Talisa to the side as she bombarded her way into the condo. "Where is Genesis?"

"He isn't here, and you need to get the hell out!"

"I'm not going anywhere until I speak with Genesis." Denise was setting the mood for a showdown. "So you're the hussy he traded me in for, black eye and all. Don't you have a man?"

"Yeah, his name is Genesis, now get the fuck out!"

Denise glanced up at Talisa, who was around four inches taller than her. She pondered for a few seconds if she could take her down strictly using her fists. Not wanting to take any chances she pulled out the knife she kept in her purse.

"Now who is your man again?" Denise asked, flashing the sharp object in Talisa's direction.

Talisa backed up, grasping that she was dealing with an unstable individual. "You need to relax. Obviously you and Genesis have a lot of shit to work out, but none of it has to do with me."

"Oh, that's not the song you were singing a minute ago. What happened to 'My man is Genesis', huh? You see I'm carrying a tool and shit and decide to switch up your program. What I'm tryna to understand is why you had to come and mess up my situation. You had yourself a baller. That nigga had you walking around with a personal bodyguard. Yo' shit was straight. That wasn't enough for you. Yo' selfish ass had to come and mess up my happy home."

As Denise came closer and closer towards Talisa, it was evident she wasn't playing with a full deck. Denise had rage in her eyes and it was all directed in one person's direction. Talisa knew she had to react fast before Denise lunged at her and drew blood. Talisa reached for the vase on the table and threw it at Denise before hauling ass into the bedroom and locking the door. The vase missed hitting Denise and crashed onto the Brazilian walnut hardwood floor.

"Don't you run away from me!" Denise screamed. She began stabbing her knife into the door and using her body to push it at the same time. For such a little woman, her fury gave her superhuman strength.

Talisa grabbed the cordless phone off the dresser and dialed Genesis's cell number. It was going straight to voice mail. She wrestled with the idea of calling the police, but had a pretty good idea that Genesis dabbled in illegal activity and didn't want to bring any unnecessary heat on him. Right when Talisa was about to dial Genesis's number again, she heard his voice:

"Yo,' what the fuck is wrong wit' you, Denise?"

Denise was frozen, with the knife stuck in the door. She struggled to get it out but, Genesis came over and knocked her hand off of it, pulling it out

"Yo' ass is crazy!" Genesis pointed his finger in her face. "Now get the fuck out my crib and don't you ever come back!"

"How can you do this? You played me, sending me back to Philly so you can be in LA wit' yo' new bitch. Bringing her here and having her sleep in the same bed we used to fuck in. You a foul nigga, Genesis."

"Denise, you need to go now. I ain't neva promised you shit and I don't owe you shit. This my motherfuckin' crib and you wasn't nothin' but a visitor. Now get the fuck out before I toss your crazy ass over that balcony outside!"

"I'm leaving, but best believe you gon' get yours, motherfucker. I promise you that shit."

Genesis was fuming as he watched Denise break out. It was a situation like this that tested his self control because everything inside of him wanted his fist to crack her jaw. She had not only disrespected his space, but also his girl.

"Talisa, are you straight?" he asked, knocking on the bedroom door.

"I'm good," Talisa said, opening the door.

Genesis held Talisa in his arms feeling completely responsible for getting her caught up in his "Diary of a Mad Black Woman" drama. "I can't believe Denise came over here trippin' like that. I'm sorry that you had to deal with that bullshit."

"Genesis, you all must've been pretty serious for her to come at me like that," Talisa assumed, releasing herself from Genesis's arms.

"I swear it wasn't like that, at least not in my mind. We've been kicking it for a few months but it was on some no strings attached type shit."

"Then why would she think it was something more?"

"I don't know. I mean, before we went to LA I did suggest she leave some of her clothes over here because she was spending the night a few times a week, but it's not like I told her to move in."

"But you gave her the impression that might be the next step?"

"Maybe, I guess. But that still don't give her the right to come to my fuckin' crib swinging a knife around and threatening you. She's a psycho. I ain't sign on for that."

"Do you think she's coming back?"

"I'm letting the security downstairs know if they see her across the street to call the cops on her silly ass. But I ain't trippin' off Denise. She'll find a new man to stalk and forget all about me."

"I wouldn't be so sure about that. Her threats seemed genuine to me."

"For her sake she betta not be that stupid. Everybody can be dealt with, including Denise."

Chapter Fourteen
I'm That Chick

"Damn, baby! Can't nobody suck me off the way you do," Arnez said, rubbing on Chanel's round brown breasts.

Chanel glanced up at him and smiled after swallowing his cum. "I told you I'm the only bitch you need. Can't nobody satisfy you like me."

"I know. Why you think I keep you around?" Arnez smirked, smacking Chanel's spectacular ass.

"Does that mean your done playing footsy with Talisa and ready to settle down with a real woman like me?"

"In due time." Arnez reached for a cigarette and lighter from his nightstand. "I have some unfinished business to handle with Talisa before I move on with anybody."

"Do you have any idea where she went?"

"I have my people checking around. I'm thinking maybe she went back to her parents in New York, but

I'm not sure yet."

"What about Genesis."

"What about him?"

"Remember I called you that night after the shooting and told you they were stashed up in the hotel together?"

"Yeah, but that was a one-time thing. Talisa hasn't been in contact wit' that nigga since. I kept my eye on that. I saw that cat in LA a few weeks ago and he had some other bitch wit' him. He ain't fuckin' wit' Talisa."

"It wouldn't hurt to check, 'cause the same night your girl got missing he had been at the crib visiting CoCo."

"Genesis was in Atlanta?"

"Yep, and I don't believe in coincidences."

"You might be onto something." Arnez thought back to the day when he came back to the hotel in LA and Talisa was packing up her belongings and telling him she was leaving. At the time he thought she was in one of her rebellious moods, but maybe she had actually hooked up with Genesis and got the balls up to bounce.

"I definitely think you need to look into it."

"Where does Genesis live?"

"In Philly."

"Do you know exactly where?"

"I don't, but CoCo probably has the address since they close and shit."

"I want you to also find out everything you can about the girl I saw him with in LA. If he is fuckin' around wit' Talisa, ain't nothin' like a scorned woman. Do you think Genesis would tell CoCo if Talisa is staying wit' him?"

"He might, but he seems to be private when it comes to his personal life. I can see what I can find out and also get what you need on that chick he was with in LA. I'm already putting the pressure on CoCo on that other shit. I don't want to push too hard though. But I might have another person I can get the info from."

"How is shit coming along with CoCo? Is she biting the bullet or what?"

"She mos def shook. First, the shooting at your party, and then having your man kill Chuck. I think that pushed her over the edge. She's this close to being ready to get out the game. Then I can take over and you can get the direct connect. With those prices and CoCo out the loop, you'll have everything on lock. You'll truly be reigning supreme as the king of this drug operation."

"That's right, and you'll be right next to me on the throne. Now come over here and give me some of that pussy."

"My pleasure, daddy!"

****

"Deuce, you still ain't heard from Antwon?" Genesis asked, pacing the floor.

"Nope, and his battery must've died 'cause it's going straight to voice mail all day."

"Damn, what the fuck is up wit' that? So when is the last time you actually spoke to him?"

"When he reached his destination, hung out wit' his people, and was on his way back." Genesis knew that meant he made it to Memphis, met up with the Fed-Ex guy, and got the drugs.

"A'ight, well keep me posted. Get back to me the moment you hear anything from that nigga."

"Got you."

"Fuck, I don't need this bullshit right now!" Genesis barked, tossing his phone down.

"Baby, is everything okay?" Talisa could clearly see from his body language that it wasn't.

"One of my main dudes is ghost. He went to pick up some shit and we shoulda heard from that nigga by now. *I pray he didn't get popped,*" Genesis said under his breath.

"Has this ever happened before, you know, him not calling?"

"Nah, he be on top of his shit." Genesis went over to the bar and poured himself a drink. "This shit becoming entirely too fuckin' stressful. I just need to stack enough paper and break out this bullshit before it breaks me."

"How much money do you need? I mean, from the look of things you're not hurting for nothing."

"I not, but it's much easier to maintain this lifestyle when it's tax free and the cash is flowing then when the government come in and yank half your shit. See, them top notch corporate motherfuckers know all the tricks and trades to maneuver out that shit, but I don't have those type of connections. At the end of the day if my money ain't legit, I'm just another street nigga."

"Is that what you want?"

"Do I want what?"

"To be a legitimate businessman."

"Hell yeah! If I can still live the life I'm accustomed to and have my baby do the same," he said, stroking the side of Talisa's face. "Doing without the stress of dealing with the shenanigans in this here drug trade may alleviate some premature gray hairs from sneaking up on me."

"Then do it. Become legitimate."

"Baby girl, if it was only that easy. You know how many niggas wouldn't be serving football numbers right now in the federal penitentiary if we could turn our illegal riches into justifiable income? It ain't like that for the typical nigga out here hustling in the streets. We don't have those types of relationships like them rich white boys do."

"But what if you did?"

Genesis gave Talisa a peculiar stare. "I'm not following you."

"What if I could introduce you to someone that could make that happen for you?"

"That would have to be a pretty powerful person and a very good friend of yours to even consider doing that for me. No offense, baby, but I don't see you knowing that type of individual. But I appreciate you wanting to help out."

"How about you take a trip with me to New York."

"What, you want to do some shopping?"

"No, I want you to meet my father."

Genesis put his drink down and took Talisa's hand. "I guess that means you've decided you do want to stay with me. I can't believe I worked my magic that fast."

"You're so arrogant, Genesis," Talisa laughed. "I do want to stay with you but that's not why I want you to meet my father."

"Then why?"

"Because he's the man that has the power and is a very good friend of mine," Talisa disclosed, ready to present a convincing case.

"I'm confused. You coming all the way from left field with this one. Who the fuck is your father?"

"Jeffery Washington."

"That name sounds familiar."

"It should, he's the owner of one of the largest investment firms in the country, Washington Investment Management."

"That's your father? They handle everything from stocks, bonds, mutual funds and insurance."

"Exactly. I see you know your shit."

"No doubt. I stay on top of the business section in the *Wall Street Journal*."

"Good. Then you know he's the type of businessman you need to get you where you want to go."

Genesis walked outside to the private terrace. He sat down on the club chaise lounge and put his finger on his forehead as if deep in thought.

Talisa looked on from a distance, knowing revealing who her father was threw him for a loop. But she wanted Genesis to accomplish all his dreams, and if she could assist him in making them happen, then that's what she planned on doing. She stood in the opening of the sliding doors on the terrace, waiting for him to share his thoughts with her.

After a long period of silence, Genesis finally said, "I can't believe your father is Jeffery Washington. How did you end up in Atlanta with a man like Arnez?"

"You mean a drug dealer?"

"Basically. I mean I'ma drug dealer too, so it don't make me no better except I ain't no woman beater. But you got breeding. A woman like you ain't even supposed to fuck wit' niggas like us."

"I guess it's true that when you shelter your daughters

they're drawn to everything they were told is bad for them, which includes certain type of men."

"How did your father feel about you dating Arnez?"

"He's never actually met him and I never told Arnez who my father is. My dad pretty much stays out of my personal life. But when I stayed out of school this semester and moved to Atlanta he was disappointed. He didn't give me a hard time, but I know how much education means to him."

"Did you tell him you were living with Arnez?"

"Yes, and my parents tried several times to come to Atlanta to meet him or have me bring Arnez to New York, but I was too ashamed. He would feel like a failure if he knew I was allowing a man to beat up on me."

"Does he know you're no longer with him?"

"I had left my parents a message and I finally spoke to my father yesterday. I didn't go into details. I told them I was no longer living in Atlanta and was visiting a friend in Philadelphia. I also promised that I would come to visit them very soon. So are you going to help me keep that promise?"

"So now I'm just your friend?"

"What do you want to be, my boyfriend?"

"That, and so much more." Genesis pulled Talisa down on the chaise lounge and held her close to his chest and kissed her. He lifted her chin up so they would be eye-to-eye. "Is it okay for me to fall in love with you?"

"Of course! Why would you ask me something like that?"

"You're a pampered princess, a real one, not some manufactured hood rat version. I might be out of my league fuckin' around wit' you."

"Don't say that. You're special, Genesis. I knew that from the moment I met you. Please don't look at me any differently because of who my father is or how I grew up. I have the same issues and problems like any other twenty-one year old female out here trying to find herself. My father just happens to be extremely wealthy, that's all."

Genesis stopped any further conversation by quieting Talisa with a profound kiss. He wanted her to sense how deep his feelings went for her.

Talisa pressed her body closer to his, wanting to give into her passion at that very moment, and she did.

The two made love right then outside on the private terrace as the sun set.

Chapter Fifteen
Prelude To Death

"Tomorrow we're off to New York to meet the parents. Are you ready?"

"Talisa, I was ready a couple of weeks ago. You the one stalling and shit."

"Don't even try it, Genesis. If I remember correctly, you were so damn happy when Antwon reappeared and everything was straight, you wanted to stay here and make some money. How soon we forget."

"Watch your mouth, little girl," Genesis shook his finger as if scolding Talisa. "I mean, shit, I had to handle my business. All that product Antwon was carrying equals serious loot. I couldn't break outta town and enjoy myself without making sure it was distributed properly."

"All that's cool, just don't try to say it was me stalling when it was all you. You're wrong on this one, so don't get slick."

"I'll show you slick," Genesis said, tickling Talisa profusely as she squirmed in bed.

"Stop it!" She laughed so hard her stomach began cramping. "Genesis, stop, pleeeeease!" Talisa pleaded.

"Not until you say I was right and you're wrong." Genesis paused and waited for Talisa to respond.

"I'm not saying that. You were totally wrong."

"Have it your way," Genesis persisted, going back in for the kill.

"Okay, okay, *okay!* You were right and I was wrong. Now please stop tickling me. You're making my stomach hurt," Talisa belted out between laughs.

"Good decision, 'cause I was prepared to tickle you until you pissed on yourself."

"Genesis, you're the worst!"

"No I'm not." He kissed Talisa on the tip of her nose. "Regardless, you love me," Genesis joked.

"You're right, I do," Talisa acknowledged, becoming serious.

"Are you saying what I think you're saying? Because once you say it, I'm not gonna let you take it back."

"I don't want to take it back. Genesis Taylor, I'm in love with you."

"Talisa Washington, I'm in love with you too, baby."

****

Arnez arrived at the Philadelphia International Airport with one objective—to teach Talisa a lesson she would never forget. He went outside and his hired help was waiting in a black Navigator to drive him to his first destination.

Chanel, being the loyal soldier that she was to Arnez, got all the information he needed through a simple flirtatious phone call conversation with Deuce.

At first Arnez was devastated when it was confirmed that not only was Talisa involved with Genesis, but they were living together. He felt betrayed in the worse way and wanted Talisa dead. But after the initial anger subsided, he believed that death would be a much too easy punishment for her and had something much more sinister in mind.

When the driver pulled up in the parking lot of the apartment complex on 400 Presidential Blvd., Arnez didn't waste any time. "You stay here. I'll be back shortly."

The driver nodded his head as Arnez shut the back door. He walked over to the ground-level apartment number that was given to him by Chanel. He knocked and waited but there was no answer. He knew this was the address Chanel gave him and wondered if maybe she had made a mistake. But that would've surprised Arnez being how thorough Chanel was when it came to following through on his orders. Arnez knocked again and he heard someone unlocking the door.

"Can I help you?" Denise asked with a towel wrapped around her body.

"Denise, right?" Arnez recognized her distinctive face from that night at the party.

"Who are you and how do you know my name?" she eyed the well-dressed handsome man up and down. He did look somewhat familiar.

"My name is Arnez." He reached out his hand but Denise

wouldn't shake it.

"Look, I just got out the shower and I'm running late for work. You need to tell me what you want quickly, 'cause I gotta go."

"I understand, but I think I can make this worth your time."

Denise still wasn't budging until Arnez opened up his wallet revealing nothing but loads of hundred dollar bills. She hadn't seen that type of cash since her days of messing around with Genesis. After kicking her to the curb it was back to working countless hours at the retail store and dealing with corner hustlers who would nickel and dime her all to keep her bills paid.

"What did you say your name was again?" Denise eyes were now sparkling.

"Arnez."

"Come on in, Arnez. Have a seat while I put some clothes on."

Arnez looked around the cute but modest apartment knowing that Denise would be thirsty enough to take the bait. He sat down on the chair until Denise came out wearing a jogging suit. "That was fast."

"Like I told you, I'm running late for work. But you said you'll make it worth my time, which I don't have a lot of," Denise said, being antsy.

"Here, take this. Maybe it'll help you relax." Arnez slipped five bills in Denise's hand and she immediately sat up straight giving Arnez her full attention.

"What the fuck is this about? You recruiting prostitutes or somethin'? Did Latrice that work at the beauty salon on Broad Street give you my address?"

"No, I don't know a Latrice and I'm not recruiting prostitutes, but I do need your services."

"What kind of services?"

"You know a gentleman by the name of Genesis?"

"What, you a friend of his? He got you over here paying me off so what, I'll leave him alone? Fine, you did your job. I got your money. Tell that motherfucker I won't call his phone no more. Now goodbye!" Denise stood up shooing Arnez out her apartment.

"Sit back down."

"No, you sit up and get out. I ain't got time for this. If I knew you were friends with Genesis, I woulda neva let you in my crib."

"I'm not a friend of Genesis. Now sit down!" His authoritative tone rattled Denise for a second and she sat down feeling uneasy. "Now calm down and listen."

"Okay."

"As I'm sure you know, Genesis is now living with a woman named Talisa."

"Oh snap, that's where I know you from! You were at T-Roc's party wit' her. I knew you looked familiar. What, you want to get wit' me on some payback shit to your ex?"

"No, I wanted to use an approach that wasn't quite so juvenile."

"I'm puzzled. If you don't want to use me to get your ex jealous, then what?"

"All I need for you to do is to find out where Genesis will be tonight and let me know."

"That's it?"

"That's it. Do you think you can handle that?"

"Yeah, he always goes to the same place every Wednesday

night. But why do you want to know where Genesis is going to be? Are you tryna fight the nigga?"

"No, again I don't want to use a juvenile approach. I just want an opportunity to speak with Talisa alone. I've tried calling her but she won't pick up."

"I know how that is. I haven't been able to get Genesis on the phone since we left LA. One minute this nigga got me on cloud nine, next he traded me in for your chick. What type of sense does that make?"

"Absolutely none. That's why I'm hoping if I have a chance to see Talisa away from Genesis, she'll realize that I'm the only man for her, and she'll come back to Atlanta with me."

"You think that might really work?"

"That's my hope. Talisa and I share a strong history together. It's the sort of bond that can't easily be broken. Talisa is young and I'm thinking maybe she's rebelling, having some fun."

"Yeah, she's having fun on my expense. Genesis was damn near about to wife me until Talisa came along."

"So are you willing to help me out? Hey it can be a win-win for you. I'll get Talisa out of town and that will leave the door wide open for you to rekindle your relationship with Genesis."

"That's true."

"And, I'll add another g to that. Fifteen-hundred dollars for a location and a chance to get rid of Talisa for good. I'm willing to guarantee whatever job you have to rush off to ain't putting that type of cash in your pocket."

Denise couldn't argue with that. "Lets say I did tell you where Genesis will be tonight and you were able to get

Talisa to leave town wit' you. There is no guarantee she won't go back to Genesis."

"Trust me, with your help, after tonight you won't ever have to worry about Talisa and Genesis getting back together again."

Denise weighed her options, and it wasn't brain surgery for her to figure out what she wanted to do. With Talisa out of the picture she did reason that there was hope for her and Genesis. As far as Denise was concerned, Talisa had a great catch with Arnez. He had looks, money and seemed to care a great deal about her to go through all these changes to win her back. Denise didn't think it was fair for Talisa to have both men vying for her affection while she was left destitute and manless.

"I'm down," Denise agreed and showed her devotion for their mutual cause by sticking out her hand.

Arnez willingly added another ten bills to his "destroy Talisa" fund. He was so eager to see his plan come to fruition, Denise could've named any price and Arnez would've gladly obliged.

"Now, I need to sit down and have a conversation with Talisa. What type of head game is she workin' wit' that got you dropping all this money so you can have a chance to speak wit' her in private? I could surely learn a thing or two from homegirl."

"Denise, back to the information."

"Can't forget that. Every Wednesday night, Genesis and his partner, Deuce go to Buffalo Billiards on Chestnut to shoot pool."

"Are you positive they will be there tonight?"

"Unless that shit close down. It's a ritual for them. During the months I dated him, they never missed a night."

"What time do they usually go and what model car will Genesis be in?"

"Seven, and Genesis is very punctual so I'm sure he'll be there right on time. He usually drives one of his everyday cars, either the black Range Rover or black Benz. He keeps his real expensive whips parked and only takes them out for special occasions. You know he don't want to draw too much unnecessary attention to himself."

"Denise, thank you. You have no idea how helpful you've been."

"I should be thanking you. If you can get Talisa to take you back and get on the next flight to Atlanta, that might put me in the driver's seat. Maybe then Genesis will see I'm the woman he needs."

"I'm sure he will," Arnez gassed Denise so she would continue to believe her own hype. He loved women like her because they followed the money trail every time. It didn't matter how shameful the road they had to travel.

****

Tonya was in the kitchen making fried chicken, macaroni and cheese and mashed potatoes for Deuce's two eldest boys with his first baby mama, as they played NBA Ballers: Chosen One on the Xbox 360. For the second time this week his baby mama had an excuse as to why she wouldn't be able to pick the boys up from school, so Deuce had to. Of course he wasn't about to let his parental obligations stop his flow, so he dropped them off at the crib leaving them with Tonya.

Tonya was growing increasingly tired of her babysitting duties. She was beginning to feel not only like a slave for Deuce, but also for his children. At least every other weekend all four of his children by three different women would stay at the crib, and of course Tonya was the one who had to watch over them. She had to perform all the wifely duties—cook, clean, suck and fuck without any wifely benefits.

Without meaning to, Tonya had fallen hard for Deuce and hated to admit it, but was in love with the dude. She had also grown attached to his crumb-snatcher kids. But being locked down like this with no form of real commitment from Deuce was not the life she had envisioned for herself. She had now reached a crossroads in her relationship with Deuce and it was time for him to either put up or shut up.

"Hey baby, the food smelling good up in here," Deuce said, sneaking up behind Tonya while she was preparing the boys' plates.

"Thanks," she said bitterly. "Do you want me to make you a plate too?"

"No, I'm good. You know I'm leaving in a few to meet Genesis."

"That's right, it's pool night. So are you taking the boys wit' you?"

"Actually, Shaniqua called and she working late tonight, so she need the boys to spend the night wit' me."

"How convenient for the both of you!" Tonya snapped.

"Baby, don't be like that." Deuce tried to kiss on Tonya's neck but she walked off.

"Come on Terrell and Lamont, your food is ready." Tonya put their plates on the dining room table and walked back into the kitchen to get their glasses of juice.

"Tonya, I know you be holding it down for me and my kids, and baby, I really do appreciate it."

"I can't tell," Tonya rolled her eyes.

"Well, maybe this will convince you."

Tonya almost dropped the two glasses she was carrying when her eyes saw the five-karat princess cut diamond sparkling from the little black box.

"Is that what I think it is?" Tonya was stunned, refusing to take her eyes away from the diamonds. She put the glasses down to further inspect the most beautiful ring she had ever seen.

"It sure is. I wanted to wait until this weekend and do the whole romantic dinner by candlelight proposal thing, but by how moody you've been I was worried you wouldn't stay around that long." They both laughed finding the humor in how true that was.

"But seriously, all jokes to the side." Deuce got down on bended knee. "Tonya Price, will you marry me?"

"Yes, of course! I love you and all your damn kids!" Tonya cried as tears flowed down her face.

"I love you too, baby." Deuce slid the ring on Tonya's finger and that scared, nervous feeling he believed would come over him at the idea of being a married man didn't happen. In fact, knowing he was marrying a woman that had his back gave him a sense of peace and gratefulness.

****

CoCo was driving in her Range Rover on a late night visit to the beauty salon to get her weave tightened up when her cell phone rang from an unknown caller.

"Hello," she answered, turning down the music blaring from Usher's CD, "Here I Stand".

"It's me." CoCo instantly recognized the male voice of her informant who worked in the federal system. He always kept her posted on what was going on behind the scenes—who was hot on the fed's radar and who was snitching and cutting deals on the low. He kept CoCo in the federal drug game loop and she paid him handsomely for it.

"What's up?" She knew it couldn't be anything good for him to be calling on this particular cell phone at this time of night. She had two phones; one for play and one strictly for business.

"I got word earlier today that you've been indicted under seal along with a man named Genesis Taylor."

"What!" CoCo slowed down her driving and pulled over to the side of the road. How?"

"Do you know a man by the name of Antwon Walker?"

"Yeah, he works for Genesis."

"A couple of weeks ago he was busted in Memphis, caught with some major product. Investigators convinced him to talk and he agreed to cooperate. He gave the feds enough information to add both of you to the indictment."

"But Antwon isn't locked up, he's out on the streets."

"Yes, I'm sure he is being used as an informant."

"When are they going to arrest us?"

"I'm not sure. But do what you have to do. I have to go now."

The phone went *"click"* and CoCo wanted to vomit. She knew she had to leave Atlanta and lay low until she lawyered up. She also had to warn Genesis that he had a snitch in his crew. She dialed Genesis's number but he wasn't answering, and continued to call him, still getting no answer.

Let me call Deuce. I'm sure he knows where Genesis is, she thought to herself.

"Hello," Deuce answered.

"Hi Deuce, it's me CoCo."

"What's good, CoCo?"

"I'm trying to get in touch with Genesis but he ain't answering his phone. It's important I speak to him."

"I'm on my way to meet him at the pool hall now. I'll make sure he calls you."

"Please do. Tell him it's urgent." CoCo hung up with Deuce and turned her truck around as she headed back to her crib, abandoning her hair appointment. As bad as she needed her tracks tightened, her weave was no longer a priority. Getting out of town was.

****

Genesis was about to start his second game when Deuce and Antwon finally showed up to the pool hall. "Damn, niggas! Can't ya ever show up on time for anything?"

"Cut me some slack," Deuce said, elbowing Genesis. "I

got engaged today. I'ma be a married man."

"Nigga, stop bullshitting!" Genesis wasn't convinced Deuce was being straight up.

"I'm serious. I popped the question today and Tonya accepted. Honest."

"Antwon, did you know about this?"

"He broke the sad news on the car ride over."

"Congratulations man! I'm happy for you and Tonya. We have to celebrate. Deuce is officially throwing in his player card."

"Yeah, my days of whoring around are over. But Genesis, you know I want you to be my best man."

"I would be honored." Genesis turned around towards the bartender and yelled out," Everybody, my best friend is getting married! Drinks are on me!" All the patrons stood up, clapping and whistling.

"It's only going to be you and Antwon left to spread the love to the ladies."

"Make that Antwon. I'm going to New York tomorrow to meet Talisa's parents. She's the one. I know it. Pretty soon I believe we'll be walking down the aisle."

"Man, you haven't even known her long enough to say some shit like that."

"Deuce you crazy. Sometimes you just know when you've found your soul mate and I believe that's what Talisa is to me."

"I can't argue with that. Love is a strange thing."

"Can't we get off this love subject? This is supposed to be a fellas night out, remember?"

"We hear you, Antwon. No more talk about our ladies. Let's play pool. I'm ready to kick both yo' ass anyway. But first let me go pay this tab. I see the bartender over there giving me the eye. I don't want him to think I'ma try to stiff the bill," Genesis said, reaching for his wallet.

"Before I forget, CoCo was trying to get in touch wit' you. She said she tried to call you but you weren't picking up your phone."

Genesis patted his front and back pockets. "Damn, I left that shit in the car. I'll call her when we leave here."

"She said it was urgent."

"Deuce, will you go to my car and get my phone, while I pay this bill?"

"No problem. I'll be right back."

"Antwon, here," Genesis handed him the key. "That nigga probably in a daze from getting ready to tie the knot. He forgot the car keys.

"See, that's what being locked down to a woman will do to you; make you lose your mind. I'll be back."

****

Talisa was coming out of the beauty supply store after buying some hair products she needed before she left for New York with Genesis when her cell phone started ringing. The call was coming from a 215 area code and she wondered who it could be.

"Hello."

"Right now as I'm relaxing in my hotel room speaking to you, your man Genesis is about to die."

"Arnez, you sick sonofabitch, leave me and Genesis the

hell alone! I don't have time for your games or lies."

"You know I don't lie about things that are important to me. At first, I was going to kill you, but then that would take away all the joy of watching you suffer—continuously. Besides, I still love you, Talisa. After I punish you unmercifully I'll be able to forgive your indiscretion."

"I hate you! Stay away for me and Genesis!" she yelled in the phone.

"You don't get it. Genesis is dead. Now start packing up your shit. You're coming back to Atlanta with me."

The confidence in Arnez's voice had Talisa in a panic. She hit the end button on her phone not able to stand the sound of his evil voice any longer.

"Pick up the phone, Genesis!" Talisa screamed, dialing his number. The phone rang and rang but Genesis didn't answer. Her hands were shaking and she could barely hit the talk button again or open the car door.

"Dear God, please don't do this to me, don't take Genesis out my life!" she cried out, struggling to put the key in the ignition. Talisa dialed his number repeatedly to no avail. She headed to Buffalo Billiards where Genesis was supposed to be. She prayed Arnez was playing a sick joke on her as tears streamed down her face while she drove to the pool hall. When she heard her cell phone ringing she quickly picked it up hoping it was Genesis returning her call, but instead it was Arnez calling back to further taunt her. She threw the phone on the passenger seat, speeding to reach her destination.

When she turned onto Chestnut she could see the flashing lights coming from the police cruisers and ambulances. Her heart was racing as she parked the car and quickly ran up to where an on-scene ranking investigative officer was sectioning off the area with yellow crime scene tape. The crime lab personnel had already placed a barrier around the body, but Talisa was determined to see if the victim was Genesis and if he was dead or alive.

She ran around to the side where a pair of emergency medical technicians were putting a man on a stretcher and were about to cover his body. Right before the sterile sheet was put over him, she caught a glimpse of the bullet hole in the back of his head, but couldn't see his face.

"Wait, that might be my boyfriend!" Talisa screamed out to the technicians carrying his body.

"Miss, you need to step back," the technician directed.

"Please, can I just see if that's my boyfriend?"

The technician reluctantly lifted the sheet, and to Talisa's relief it wasn't Genesis, nor did she recognize the dead man's face.

"Is it him?" the technician inquired.

"No, thank God!"

"The emergency crew is working on another victim over there," the technician pointed at the front entrance of the pool hall, not wanting to get Talisa's hopes up in case the other victim was her boyfriend.

Talisa ran towards the circle of people in front of the entrance and tried to break through the crowd.

"Sir, you're going to have to move," Talisa heard a paramedic insist. Poking her head between people in the crowd, Talisa could see a man lying on the ground holding his chest and trying to speak to someone who was holding his hand.

"Man, you my heart—you know that!"

"Shhh! Don't speak. Save your strength. You gon' get through this. We've been through worse together."

"Nah, this it for me. I ain't got no more free passes."

When Talisa finally broke through the crowd, she saw it was Deuce who was lying on the ground, barely alive.

"Don't say that man. You gon' make it, you got to!" Genesis was trying to be strong as he watched his best friend dying right in front of him, and his emotions took over. One tear rolled down his face as he felt the life leaving Deuce's body.

"Tell Tonya and the kids that I love them..." were Deuce's final words.

Chapter Sixteen
Last Kiss

Denise had woken up with a smile on her face and newfound hope. If the scheme Arnez orchestrated went the way it was supposed to, then Talisa was on a flight back to Atlanta or about to get on one. Arnez had promised to call and give her an update and Denise had been prancing around the apartment all day waiting to hear the magic words, "Talisa is gone!"

Denise was sitting on the couch watching "Young and the Restless" and eating her favorite cereal, Lucky Charms, when Monica came through the door looking distraught.

"Girl, is everything okay? You seem a bit flustered," Denise said dismissively before turning her attention back to the drama going on between Victor Newman and his ex-wife, Nikki, and crunching on her cereal.

"You must ain't heard." Monica sat down on the couch

and cut the television off.

"Why you turn off the 'Young and the Restless'? Victor was about to light Nikki's ass up."

"Girl, fuck that damn soap opera! Antwon and Deuce got killed last night over there at Buffalo Billiards."

Denise put her bowl down on the table and swallowed hard before speaking. "Is Genesis okay?"

"Yeah, physically, but you know mentally that nigga fucked up. You know how close he and Deuce was. And man, Tonya is distraught. I just left from over there. What make it so bad was they got engaged last night and now that nigga gone. And his kids... damn!" Monica kept shaking her head.

"Does anybody know what happened?"

"They were outside Billiards by Genesis's car and supposedly two men walked up and started blasting. They ain't made no arrest though. But ain't that the scenario for all these killings out here in Philly? Niggas die and nobody gets caught—a repetitive cycle."

"But it wasn't supposed to happen like that! I swear it wasn't!" Denise said becoming hysterical.

"Denise, what the fuck are you talking about?"

"That lying motherfucker said he only wanted time alone to speak with Talisa. You know, to win her back. And then with Talisa out the picture I would have a chance to be with Genesis again," Denise rambled, sounding as if she was hyperventilating and her entire body was trembling.

"Denise, calm down." Monica sat down next to Denise and held her arms firmly. "Look at me." Denise started taking deep breathes to relax and focus. "Now tell me what happened."

"Talisa's ex-boyfriend, Arnez came to see me yesterday."

"He came here?"

"Yes."

"How did he get your address?"

"I don't know. But he remembered me from being with Genesis at the party in LA and I saw him with Talisa. He said he only wanted to speak with Talisa and convince her that she should go back to Atlanta and be with him."

"Okay, so what does this have to do with what happened to Deuce and Antwon?"

"I think they were killed by mistake."

"What makes you think that?"

"Because Arnez asked me where Genesis was going to be last night and what type of car he would be driving, and I told him. But he gave me fifteen-hundred dollars. I didn't know he was planning on killing him. I love Genesis! I woulda never did no shit like that to him!"

"Oh shit!" Monica leaned back on the couch. "Denise, what have you done?"

Denise lifted her legs onto the couch and pulled them to her chest, wrapping her arms around them tightly. She rocked back and forth, overwhelmed that although she didn't pull the trigger, she unwittingly played a role in the death of two innocent men.

****

Talisa stood in the living room watching as Genesis sat outside on the balcony, mourning the loss of both of his friends. She wanted to console him but knew nothing she'd say could ease his pain. She still hadn't told him that Arnez was behind the brutal murders. He was so distraught that he didn't even think to ask her why she showed up. There was dead silence in the car as she drove them home, and it remained that way even now.

As Talisa was in deep thought she heard Genesis's cell phone going off. It had been ringing nonstop all morning and afternoon and mainly from a 404 area code. She looked at the phone and again and it was the same number. Following her gut instincts, this time she answered the call.

"Hello."

"Umm, maybe I dialed the wrong number," CoCo said, looking at the screen on her phone, but clearly she did not. "I'm trying to get in touch with Genesis."

"You have the right number."

"Yeah, I see that, but who are you and why are you answering Genesis's phone?"

"This is his girlfriend."

"His who?" Jealousy ripped through CoCo.

"His girlfriend. Genesis isn't available right now. Do you want to leave a message for him?"

What CoCo really wanted to do was reach through the phone and smack the crap out of whoever was playing wifey to the man she had deep feelings for. But she knew what she had to tell Genesis was too vital to let her jealousy get in the way.

"My name is CoCo, and I do business with Genesis. I need to warn him about a serious problem, so I need to speak with him now."

Talisa knew exactly who CoCo was and wondered if

any of this had to do with Arnez. "Of course. Hold on one second."

"Thanks." CoCo tried hard not to sound salty but she was dying to know who the woman was on the other end of the phone.

Talisa opened the door to the balcony and she could tell Genesis didn't want to be disturbed, but from the sound of CoCo's voice she knew he would have to be.

"CoCo is on the phone and she needs to speak with you."

"Tell her I'll call her back later."

"She said it's urgent. I think you need to speak with her."

"Give me the phone." Talisa handed Genesis the phone and went back inside.

"What is it, CoCo?"

"What's with the icy attitude? I've been trying to get in touch with you since last night. Deuce didn't give you my message?"

"Yeah he gave it to me."

"What, it's like that? You don't feel the need to return my calls anymore even when I say it's an emergency?"

"Yo', Deuce got killed last night. I can't deal wit' your smart ass mouth right now."

"Genesis, I had no idea! I'm so sorry. What happened?"

"I don't wanna talk about it right now."

"I understand."

"Now what is so urgent?"

"I hate to give you more bad news, but both of us are under a sealed federal indictment. An informant of mine who works in the federal system told me last night."

"What? When the bullshit start coming it don't stop."

"Tell me about it. And so you know, it's one of your own

who fucked us over."

"Who?"

"Antwon. He got popped on that trip to Memphis and snitched on us. He's an informant for the feds. I don't know how much information he's given them on you, but stay the hell away from that nigga."

"That won't be hard to do, since he is dead too."

"Word? Not to speak ill of the dead even if they were a snitch, but that might be a good thing as far as our case goes. But I'm not taking any chances. I got some shit together and I'm leaving first thing tomorrow morning. I got a feeling the feds gon' be sneaking up on me in the next few days and I want to be long gone. I suggest you do the same. When my lawyer finds out exactly what they working with, then I'll turn myself in. But it will be on my terms."

"I feel you. Thanks for the warning and I apologize for how I came off on you."

"No apology necessary. I know how close you were to Deuce. Chuck's death hit me the same way. But listen, I need to go. I'll call you when I get situated in my new location or if I get any updates."

"Cool. Take care of yourself, CoCo."

"I will, and you do the same."

Genesis put his head down, plagued by the news CoCo dropped on him. Not only was he a wanted man, but a person he considered a close friend was responsible for his own probable demise. Antwon had done the ultimate betrayal. He broke the most important rule of the streets—*no snitching*. He had to put aside grieving over Deuce and let his survival mode kick in.

"I have to go away for awhile," Genesis said, coming in

the living room where Talisa was sitting.

"Where are you going, and when are you coming back?"

"I don't know yet."

Talisa put down her magazine and stood up. "Wait, you're leaving and you don't know when you're coming back?"

"Pretty much."

"Then I'm coming with you."

"You can't, not right now."

"Genesis, what' going on? Don't shut me out like this. I thought you said we were in this together." The nonstop emotional beating Talisa had been enduring was taking an overwhelming toll on her. The rock she wanted to be for Genesis was cracking and she could no longer keep it in check as the tears flowed.

"Baby, please don't cry." Genesis held Talisa close as she cried on his shoulder. "Things are too fucked up right now. I have to go."

"Then let me go with you."

"I can't. CoCo told me that we've been indicted by the feds. They can come arrest me at any time." Genesis sat down on the couch, reflecting on the chain of events that had him on top of the world yesterday, but now had him perplexed as to what his future would hold.

"Genesis, let's first find out what the charges are before you go on the run."

"Fuck, them charges! Them motherfuckers ain't gonna care what the charges are or if I'm guilty or innocent. All they know is that I'ma nigga who ain't had a legitimate job in years and is living good. They gon' take my shit, throw my black ass in jail, and say we got another one off the streets."

"Let me help you," Talisa pleaded.

"Baby, I know you want to help me, but I can't get locked up again. I virtually lost my whole childhood being caged up. I can't go through that again."

"Listen to me. My father can get you the best lawyers in the country. We will beat this."

"Talisa, I don't know if I want to take that chance. You don't know if your father can help me or if he would even want to. I'ma drug dealer for fuckin' sake!"

"Trust me, it won't matter. I promise my father will help you. Baby, let's try. I need you. Please, don't leave me. I know we can get through this—together."

Genesis could see the pleading in Talisa's eyes. It was that of desperation and he didn't want to let her down. "Okay, we'll leave for New York tomorrow and see what your father can do. But Talisa, I ain't making no promises. If your father can't help, then I have to do what's best for me, and that's to keep my freedom."

****

CoCo glanced around her bedroom making sure she wasn't forgetting anything. She did have what she needed most which was a duffel bag full of money. It was more than enough cash to keep her living comfortably for however long she needed to stay on the run.

Right before heading out she picked up the envelope she had left for Chanel off her bed. CoCo hadn't been able to get in touch with her sister for the last few days, and this was the only way she could tell her what was going on. From what her informant told her, Chanel wasn't listed on the indictment and hoped it would stay that way so her sister could hold it down while she was gone.

CoCo put the envelope back down on the bed and picked up the two bags she was taking with her and headed to the front door. She looked around the stunning condo that she adored so much one last time and opened the door to escape her past and start a new future.

"CoCo Armstrong, we have a warrant for your arrest! Turn around and put your hands behind your back!" the federal agent screamed.

The agent was so close up on CoCo that when he yelled, spit flew in her face. But even under those circumstances, it didn't motivate her to move. She was frozen in disbelief at the sight of several federal agents aiming guns in her direction, and with one pull of the trigger, could blow her brains out.

"Turn around!" the federal agent screamed again, but this time he forcefully turned CoCo so her back was facing him, and he placed the handcuffs around her wrists.

****

Talisa was jolted out of her sleep by loud pounding. The more she had tried to ignore the deafening sound the louder it became.

"Genesis, what's going on?" she said half asleep. But the loud noise continued and she heard no answer to her question. With another loud boom echoing through the room, she sat up. It sounded like a truck was breaking the door down. With her eyes now fully open, she looked over to the side of the bed where Genesis had been sleeping and he was gone. In his place was a note:

Dear Talisa,

I love you more than anything in this world. Please believe that. But I had to go. I couldn't take a chance and put my life in the hands of a man that I've never even met. Know that I love you and be strong while I'm gone. When the time is right, I'll send for you.

Genesis

As Talisa sat in bed absorbing each word she had just read in the letter, she heard what sounded like an explosion. She immediately balled up the letter and tossed it under the bed. A few minutes later, federal agents were standing in the bedroom doorway with guns aimed at her.

"Put your hands up! We have an arrest warrant for Genesis Taylor."

"He isn't here," Talisa said stoically.

"Search the premises!" one of the agents ordered the other agents. "Do you have any idea where we can locate Mr. Taylor?"

"No, I don't."

Talisa watched as the agents turned the place upside down, destroying the condo they shared together. But without Genesis it no longer felt like a home to her.

She gently placed her hand over her stomach, and out of all the craziness that had gone down the last couple of days, her biggest regret was not being completely honest with Genesis. She was waiting for the right time to tell him, but it never happened. Now it might be too late. Genesis had no clue that he was the intended target for last night's murder and Arnez was the monster who was to be held accountable. Once Arnez got word that Genesis was very much alive and on the run, Talisa knew he would use the opportunity to prey upon her.

But the worst part was that Talisa's life was no longer the only one in danger. Her biggest kept secret which was supposed to be a joyous surprise to be shared with Genesis, was that the love they created was now growing inside of her—their baby.

A KING PRODUCTION

Trife Life
To
Lavish

JOY DEJA KING

Prologue
Escaping the Madness
Charlotte, North Carolina The Past...

"Get the fuck outta my house!" Teresa screamed, as she stood in the entrance of the bedroom door. Teresa's initial reaction was to drag the woman lying on her back out of the bed, but seeing the horrific shock on the woman's face made her quickly reassess that decision. Teresa and the other woman both seemed to be stuck on pause, and the only person being on fast forward was the man who continued getting his stroke on as if nothing was going to stop him from busting a nutt.

"Oh shit! I'm almost there!" the man moaned, speeding up his pace as if oblivious to the fact that he had a viewing audience.

Teresa couldn't believe she was watching as her husband fucked another woman right in front of her face. Immediately, flashback images consumed her. She thought back to all the bullshit she had been enduring for the last six years.

In the beginning, Kevon seemed to be Teresa's saving grace. She had a baby girl, who was just over a year old, had no money, no job and a bleak future. The landlord had given her an eviction notice, and Teresa was going to have to go live with her mother so she and her baby wouldn't be homeless. But that never happened, because Kevon swooped in and took on the role as her man, and a father to her daughter, Genevieve. Teresa was so enamored, that when Kevon asked that she and the baby come back to live with him at his crib in Charlotte, she packed up and left Philly, the only place she had ever called home.

Teresa felt like she had died and gone to suburban heaven, when she first arrived at the handsome two-story brick house on the tree-lined street. She had grown accustomed to living in drug infested project buildings with hallways smelling like piss, and where trash replaced grass as landscaping. Inhaling the fresh, clean air in the south seemed like a life she would only daydream about, not actually live.

But Teresa's daydreaming quickly turned into a never-ending nightmare after marrying Kevon. He was no longer her saving grace, but instead the cause of her demise.

"What the fuck is you doing here? I thought you wasn't gonna be home for another hour," Kevon spit, after finally busting a nutt and pulling himself out of the stiffened woman.

Teresa's mind was so far gone with reflecting on the horrors of the past, that at first she didn't hear her husband.

"Bitch, don't you hear me talking to you?" Kevon continued.

"Nigga, fuck you!" Teresa barked, coming out her daze. "You so damn trifling, you gon' bring another woman in my house and fuck her in my bed? I'm so sick of your disrespectful bullshit, I don't know what to do!"

"I swear I had no idea he was married, or that this was your home!" the fear stricken girl who looked no more than eighteen said, pleading her case to Teresa. She jumped out of bed, scrambling to get her clothes on, in an attempt to escape without the ass whooping she assumed his wife was about to put on her.

But unbeknownst to the teeny bopper, Teresa was beginning to grow so immune to her husband's revolting behavior, that she refused to waste her energy on beating any of his women down. Plus, she believed the girl when she said she was clueless to Kevon's marital status. This here situation needed to be handled with one person—her husband.

"You ain't got to explain shit to her! This *my* house. It ain't my fault she brought her ass back home early."

Teresa stood with her eyes twitching. *This nigga is determined to have a throw-down up in this mutherfucka, and I'ma give it to him!* "Little girl, I think it's best you go. I need to deal with my husband."

The girl nodded her head in agreement with Teresa's request, and leaped up to make an exit.

"I'll call you later on," Kevon said, casually, making it clear he wasn't pressed about how pissed Teresa was.

"Ma, who was that woman that just ran up out of here?"

Teresa looked down at her seven-year-old daughter. With all the anger consuming her, she had forgotten she was there. "Genevieve, baby, she was nobody. You go to your bedroom and close the door. I got some things to handle with your father."

Genevieve looked over at her father as he stood in only his boxer shorts, before asking, "Daddy, is everything okay?"

"I'm good," he answered, pulling out a box of cigarettes from his pants pocket and grabbing a pack of matches off the dresser to light up.

"Genevieve, g'on to your room and color or something. I'll be there in a minute."

"But I'm hungry."

Teresa slit her eyes at her daughter, not in the mood for no whining. "I'ma tell you one more time to go to your room," Teresa said, in a threatening tone that Genevieve knew all too well. "I'ma make you something to eat when I'm done in here.

Now g'on!"

Genevieve looked back at her daddy, then her mom, before walking out their room. But instead of going to her bedroom like she was told, she sat down in the hallway corner, determined to find out what had her mother so angry.

"Teresa, I don't feel like hearing whateva bullshit 'bout to come out yo' mouth," Kevon said, slipping on his jeans.

"You should'a thought about that before you brought some young ass girl up in this house!"

"Oh, would it make you feel better if I would'a brought some old ass woman up in here to fuck? I mean, I'm just saying…"

"You know what, Kevon? Why don't you pack up your shit and get the fuck out. Clearly this ain't where you wanna be no more, so I think it's best you leave."

Kevon gave a low chuckle before taking a pull off the cigarette and laying it down in the ashtray. "I hope you ain't been dabbling in my stash, because only some powerful yang can have you speaking out the side of your neck like that. 'Cause I ain't going no motherfuckin' where."

"Well, you won't be staying up in here with me with this disrespectful bullshit. I'm tired, Kevon. From you getting other bitches pregnant, having ho's stashed up in apartments, to them blowing up my phone looking for you. Now, you so sloppy wit' yo' shit, you bringing broads to the place I lay my head. I can't live like this! I won't live like this!"

"Bitch, have you forgotten where I found your busted ass at? You was a broke-down ho, with not even one dollar to your name. You didn't even have enough money to buy milk or pampers for your baby. If it wasn't for me, you and Genevieve would still be in Philly, struggling just to get by. So save all that 'you can't live like this'. You better be happy you gotta place to live."

"Oh really? You don't want to leave? Then I'll leave, 'cause anything is better than this." Teresa turned to walk away, facing the fact that she was fighting a useless cause.

"Where the fuck you think you going?" Kevon yanked Teresa's arm, stopping her from walking away.

"Get the fuck off of me! I told you I'm done wit' this shit."

"Nah, we ain't done until I say we done. I been taking care of you and a child that ain't even mine, and you think you gon' just leave me? You fuckin' crazy! That's not how this shit work. I pulled you out of those projects and made an honest woman outta you, so you owe me your life just for that."

"I don't owe you shit! And if I did, I've paid my debt in full having to deal wit' all your drama over the years. Now, get the fuck off of me! I'm taking my daughter and getting the fuck outta here."

The next thing Teresa knew, she was hitting the floor from the impact of the punch Kevon landed on her face. *This nigga been cheating on me for all these years, now he wanna put his hands on me too! Aahh, hell no!* Teresa thought as she lay on the floor staring up at the man she once believed was the best thing that ever happened to her.

"You see what you made me do? I've been nothing but a provider for you and Genevieve, and this is the respect I get. That's why you gotta treat women like hos and tricks, 'cause ya' don't 'preciate nothing. But you my wife, and you will respect me."

"Kevon, get away from me! I promised myself I would neva let another man put their hands on me, and I meant that shit!"

Kevon grabbed Teresa by her hair and dragged her over near the dresser. Teresa was swinging her arms and kicking her legs, irate and scared, not knowing what Kevon was going to do next. But Kevon was undeterred.

"You think you gon' talk shit to me in my house where I pay the bills? I don't give a fuck if you caught me up in this crib everyday wit' a different bitch, you show me respect. But just like you gotta beat obedience in your children, I'ma put the fear of God in you," he said, grabbing the still lit cigarette from the ashtray.

"Kevon, no-o-o-o-o-o!" Teresa screamed out as little pieces of ashes were falling down, barely missing her exposed skin.

"Ain't no use in screaming now. You should'a thought about that shit before running off at the mouth." Kevon lifted Teresa up off the floor like a rag doll. Her petite frame dangled in the air as Kevon pointed the cigarette towards her face. "Now, where shall I leave my mark? Some place where you can constantly look at, as a reminder that you'll always be my bitch."

All anyone could hear were the gut wrenching cries of pain as Kevon mashed the cigarette into the upper right side of Teresa's left breast.

Before he released her hair and Teresa dropped to the floor, she caught a glimpse of the devilish smirk on Kevon's face. The pain was overwhelmingly excruciating, but seeing the gratified look on her husband's mug as he was leaving her there to suffer gave Teresa the strength to fight back. With his back turned, believing she was in no condition to defend herself, Teresa grabbed the marble lamp off the nightstand, and with all her might, slammed it over Kevon's head, not once, not twice, but three times.

Exhausted from using all her strength, Teresa let the lamp drop out of her hands, and when she looked up, she saw her daughter, Genevieve standing only feet away with a blank stare on her face. Teresa then looked down at Kevon, and blood was pouring from the open gash on his head.

"Oh shit, he's dead!" Teresa mumbled, as she shook his rigid body, looking for any sign of life.

"Ma, is Daddy dead? Did you kill Daddy?"

"This man here, ain't none of your Daddy," Teresa said, firmly latching onto her daughter's arm.

Genevieve's eyes filled with tears. She heard the

harsh words exchanged between her parents, but didn't want to believe they were true. Kevon was the only father she'd known, and although he didn't treat her mother well all the time, for the most part, he had been decent towards her. But now her mother was affirming the worst; Kevon wasn't her father, and now he was dead.

"I can't believe you killed my Daddy!" Genevieve said, under sniffles, still unable to call him anything else.

"Didn't you hear what I said? That man ain't none of your Daddy!" Teresa screamed, pointing to the dead body. "Now hush up with that crying! I need to think." Teresa's hands were shaking and her head throbbing. She wanted to get away from Kevon and leave him with some of the pain he had caused her, but murder was never part of the equation.

"Ma, what you gon' do?"

"You mean what *we* gon' do? We getting the hell outta here. Go to your room and pack up as much stuff you can fit in here," Teresa ordered, opening the closet door and handing her daughter a suitcase.

"But I don't wanna leave Daddy like this!" The tears were now flowing down Genevieve's face.

"Look at me. I said, look at me!" Teresa yelled, holding her daughter tightly. She knelt down on the floor so she could be eye level with Genevieve. "I know you scared, baby, so am I. But mommy had to defend herself. I didn't mean to kill Kevon, it was an accident, but the police probably wouldn't believe me. I would go to jail and they would send you away to some foster home. I don't want to lose you, baby, so we have to leave."

"And go where, Ma?"

"I'm not sure, but somewhere far away, where nobody knows us or can find us. All we have is each other now, so please, baby, don't fight me. Do what Mommy says. Go to your room and pack up your things. I'll come get you when it's time to go."

Genevieve looked over at Kevon and back into the eyes of her mother. She grabbed the suitcase and left the room.

Teresa wanted to break down and cry, not to mourn the death of her husband, but because she knew her life would never be the same again. She spent the next hour packing up her belongings and trashing the place. When Kevon's body was discovered, she hoped that it would appear as if someone had broken in looking for either money or drugs. It was known in the streets of Charlotte that Kevon was heavily involved with the drug game, and other illegal activities.

Before Teresa left, she grabbed the murder weapon and wrapped it up in a towel before putting it in one of her bags. She then went to Kevon's closet and took the money he always kept in a pair of Timberland boots. She knew Kevon had another spot where he stashed his drugs and real paper, but had no idea exactly where it was, nor did she have the time to try and figure it out. The money Teresa took wasn't enough to ball, but it would hold them over until they found a new home.

"Genevieve, it's time to go, baby," Teresa said, calmly. She held her daughter's hand and looked around the place she'd called home for years. Not only would their lives change, but so would their names. Teresa and Genevieve no longer existed, she decided, closing the door and escaping the madness.

A KING PRODUCTION

Nico Carter

Men Of The Bitch Series

JOY DEJA KING

Chapter 1

I Got A Story To Tell

I came into this world wanting one thing... love. I couldn't get that love from my mother so I stole it from the streets. Eventually, I did get the love, respect, and money I craved, but it came at a very high price. As I stand here today, I can't help but ask myself, was it worth it? But before I can answer that question and move forward, I have to go back to what brought me here.

👑 👑 👑

"Nico, get yo' ass in this house," my mother yelled out the window.

"I'm coming!" I yelled back for the third time, running with the ball in my hands, knowing I was lying again. We were playing the hood version of football and my team was winning so I didn't want to stop. See, the older boys in the neighborhood thought they could kick our ass 'cause we were young.

My boy Lance and I were only 10, but we were both tall for our age, fast, and already had a lil' muscle tone. My best friend, Ritchie, and the other boys on our team were either below average or average at best. But with Lance and my skills and the other boys just following our lead, we would constantly beat the older boys. It would drive them crazy and I loved it.

"Touch down!" I hollered and started doing my signature two-step dance move before throwing the ball down. "Peace out motherfuckers!" I grinned, before running towards my apartment.

"We see you tomorrow!" I heard Ritchie and the other boys yell back.

"Boy, you see what time it is?" my mother popped as soon as I closed the door. "You know you ain't supposed to be outside when it get this dark."

"Sorry. I was playing football and didn't realize it was so late."

"Well go in there and get yo'self cleaned up. Yo' daddy will be over here in a little bit," my mom said, fixing her hair in the mirror.

"Now it makes sense," I mumbled.

"What you say, boy?" my mother said, shooting me one of her evil looks.

"I just said I was hungry," I lied.

"I'm sure yo' daddy will take us out to eat when he gets here. So hurry up! I want you to be clean, dressed, and ready when he walk through that door."

I was wondering why my mom was so concerned about me coming in the house. Normally, I could come home at any time of the night and she wouldn't notice or care. She would assume I was at Ritchie's house or another kid in the building and it almost felt like she preferred I stayed there. The only time she wanted me around was if my father was coming over to visit. She would always put on this big show as if she was the Mother Of The Year. I would play along because part of me was always hoping that maybe one day her pretending would rub off and become a reality.

After taking a bath, I decided to put on the New York Knicks jersey my dad had gotten me. I smiled looking at myself in the mirror. I was the spitting image of my father and that made me feel proud.

"Where my lil' man Nico at!" I heard my father call out.

"What up, Dad!" I said, running up to him. He wrapped his strong arms around me giving me a hug like only he could.

"I just saw you a couple days ago and you already grew a few inches. Damn, you a handsome kid, if I say so myself." My dad smiled proudly.

"You only saying that 'cause he look just like you." My mother laughed.

"But of course. Nico know where he get them good looks from, don't you boy," my dad teased, putting his huge hand on top of my head and playfully shaking it. "You ready to go?"

"Yes, sir. Where we going?"

"I got us tickets to go see the Yankees play."

"No way!"

"Do I ever lie to you?"

"Nope, you sure don't, Daddy."

"And I never will. Now let's get outta here."

"Nico said he was hungry. I thought the three of us would go get something to eat," my mother said, folding her arms.

"Maybe next time, Shaniece. Tonight it's just me and my son," my dad said, taking my hand. When I turned to tell my mother bye, she was rolling her eyes.

"What you mean maybe next time? Don't you see me dressed? You think I got all jazzed up to sit in this apartment?"

"Here, go out and have a good time wit' your girlfriends. Nico can stay with me for the night," my dad said, giving my mother a bunch of money. She balled it up in her fist tightly, but I could tell she was steaming mad.

4

"Fine, you keep him, but you still owe me dinner," she snapped, putting her other hand on her hip.

"See you tomorrow, Mom," I said about to go give her a hug goodbye, but she walked away. I took my dad's hand and we left.

My dad had recently bought a new gold, two door Mercedes Benz sedan and this was the first time I was going for a ride in it. Last week when he stopped by so I could see it, everybody went crazy on the block. My dad was the man and when I grew up I wanted to be just like him. After we got in the car and settled in my dad turned on the radio. But before I could start jamming to the beat, he turned the music down and looked at me.

"Nico, I want you to know something," he said with a stone face. My dad was always smiling and joking so it was weird seeing him so serious.

"What is it, Dad?"

"You're my son, my only child and I love you no matter what."

"I know and I love you, too."

"You might not be seeing me around at your mother's place that much anymore, but I want you to come stay at my house on the weekends. Is that okay with you?"

"Yes! I just wanna spend time with you. I don't care where."

"That's my boy. Now let's go see these Yankees." My dad smiled and drove off.

Although I was young, I knew exactly what was going on. Ever since I could remember my mother and father were on and off. They never lived together and half the time they were arguing and the other half they were in the bedroom with the door locked. I guess they were about to be off again. My dad had never told me he wasn't going to be coming around, so something had changed, I just didn't know what.

Diamond

"Bitch, you ain't shit!" When my baby daddy stood in front of me screaming that bullshit with spit flying everywhere, I kept putting the clear coat of polish on my nails ignoring his ass. "Did you hear what the fuck I said?" he belted as the vein in the middle of his forehead started pulsating.

"Mutherfucka, everybody in the damn building can hear what the fuck you just said. Are you done ranting 'cause I got shit to do?"

"That's what's wrong wit yo' ass, yo' mouth too fuckin' slick."

"Umm this shit gettin' repetitive. Ain't but so many ways you can call me a bitch and tell me I ain't shit. I get it, you think I'm foul. So either come up with some new descriptions or move on to something else."

"I can't believe I got a baby wit' yo' stupid ass. You don't give a fuck about nobody but yourself. One day I promise I'ma take our daughter away from you because I refuse to let her grow up and end up like you."

I put my polish down and eyeballed Rico because I wanted him to know what I was about to say wasn't a game. "Nigga, the day you start plotting to take my daughter away from me is the day you better tell yo' mama to start making your funeral arrangements. You can call me every ho, dick sucker, no good bitch all mutherfuckin' day but when you bring Destiny into the mix we have a problem. Now please get the fuck out my crib and take that noise you spewing someplace else."

"Diamond, this shit ain't over. I'll be back tomorrow to pick up my daughter for the weekend and she better be here and not at your mother's house."

"I tell you what. Why don't you pick Destiny up from my mother's house tomorrow because I can't take having to see yo' ass two days in a row."

"No, I'll pick Destiny up from here tomorrow. So whatever partying and fucking you planning on doing tonight make sure you have yo' ass up in time to get my daughter in the morning."

"That's what your problem is now. So busy worrying about what the fuck I'm doing," I huffed under my breath not wanting to reignite the argument because I was ready for Rico to bounce. "Bye," I said keeping my head down, until I heard the door shut.

There was a time an argument with Rico would fuck up my entire day but this shit had become so routine I barely broke a sweat over it now. See, there was a time when Rico was actually my boyfriend. I thought we would be together forever but that was when I was young and dumb. He swooped me up when I was fifteen and not used to good dick or money. When I was walking home from school one afternoon he pulled up in a tricked out Benz and I couldn't believe when he rolled down the window asking me for my name. He was one of those pretty niggas who knew his packaging was right.

From that day on we started dating. Rico would pick me up from school almost everyday and them chick's mouths dropped every time he pulled up and I would get in the car. We would go get something to eat and just talked. Although he was three years older than me he never made me feel like a kid instead I felt like a woman. But I wasn't a woman and Rico was way out of my league. He quickly made me his girl but that didn't keep him from having mad other bitches, so many I couldn't keep count. In the beginning I fell for all his lies. He had a valid excuse for every accusation I had. By the time I woke up to the truth it was two years later and I was pregnant with Destiny.

That was the roughest nine months of my life. I had bitches calling my phone harassing me. They would say my man just left their crib and he fucked the shit out of them. My feet swelled up, belly poked out feeling depressed and helpless having to hear this shit. By this time, Rico wasn't even trying to hide his dirt anymore. He felt I was pregnant and stuck. Even after all that I stayed with Rico. It took another year before I wised up and gave that nigga the deuces. When I did Rico tried to make my life a living hell. I guess he thought I would be a dumbass forever...not!

I spent the first year of Destiny's life being with her day and night while Rico ran the streets. I don't even remember him changing one diaper. But I loved her so much it didn't even matter. Destiny was like my real life baby doll and she helped me get my shit together. I had gained so much weight during my pregnancy and even more afterwards and I think it was out of depression, because Rico had me so stressed out. I decided I had to get myself back on point and I started taking Destiny out in her stroller everyday. Within six months I had walked all that weight off. After that you couldn't tell me nothing, including Rico. I went from being a sad, miserable bitch to a baller bitch.

Get Caught Up
On The Entire Bitch Series...

P.O. Box 912
Collierville, TN 38027

www.joydejaking.com
www.twitter.com/Joydejaking

A King Production

ORDER FORM

Name:

Address:

City/State:

Zip:

QUANTITY	TITLES	PRICE	TOTAL
	Bitch	$15.00	
	Bitch Reloaded	$15.00	
	The Bitch Is Back	$15.00	
	Queen Bitch	$15.00	
	Last Bitch Standing	$15.00	
	Superstar	$15.00	
	Ride Wit' Me	$12.00	
	Ride Wit' Me Part 2	$15.00	
	Stackin' Paper	$15.00	
	Trife Life To Lavish	$15.00	
	Trife Life To Lavish II	$15.00	
	Stackin' Paper II	$15.00	
	Rich or Famous	$15.00	
	Rich or Famous Part 2	$15.00	
	Rich or Famous Part 3	$15.00	
	Bitch A New Beginning	$15.00	
	Mafia Princess Part 1	$15.00	
	Mafia Princess Part 2	$15.00	
	Mafia Princess Part 3	$15.00	
	Mafia Princess Part 4	$15.00	
	Mafia Princess Part 5	$15.00	
	Boss Bitch	$15.00	
	Baller Bitches Vol. 1	$15.00	
	Baller Bitches Vol. 2	$15.00	
	Baller Bitches Vol. 3	$15.00	
	Bad Bitch	$15.00	
	Still The Baddest Bitch	$15.00	
	Power	$15.00	
	Power Part 2	$15.00	
	Drake	$15.00	
	Drake Part 2	$15.00	
	Female Hustler	$15.00	
	Female Hustler Part 2	$15.00	
	Princess Fever "Birthday Bash"	$9.99	
	Nico Carter The Men Of The Bitch Series	$15.00	
	Bitch The Beginning Of The End	$15.00	
	Supreme...Men Of The Bitch Series (Coming February 29th, 2016)	Pre Order $15.00	

Shipping/Handling (Via Priority Mail) $6.50 1-2 Books, $8.95 3-4 Books add $1.95 for ea. Additional book.

Total: $_____FORMS OF ACCEPTED PAYMENTS: Certified or government issued checks and money Orders, all mail in orders take 5-7 Business days to be delivered